CRYSTAL CHOICE

The Second Novel in the Projector War Saga

Other books by K. A. Excell

CRYSTAL MIND

CRYSTAL CHOICE

CRYSTAL TRUTH

CRYSTAL CHOICE

The Second Novel in the Projector War Saga

K. A. Excell

For Angie, who helped me keep going.

CHAPTER ONE

I strode down the hallway of Martial Academy fast enough that Eugene Berry would have no-doubt given me detention had he been around. It wouldn't be the first time. I could still see his lips curled into a smirk as he formed my name.

"Crystal Farina. Detention—again."

After that incident, I'd taken extra care to use my new Psionic abilities to make sure that neither Berry nor any other Prefects had the satisfaction of giving me detention. Of course, detention wouldn't change a thing. I was already going to be here all weekend for a team training exercise that started on Friday. They'd been happening more and more often—which was probably good, given how tensions were rising. The Agency and the Company were at each other's throats. I was still so junior that Ms. King only smiled and told me not to worry when I asked her about it, but I couldn't ignore the way she hurried off to meetings, or the way she scanned us when she thought we weren't looking. Something was afoot, and she was worried we wouldn't be ready in time.

I arrived outside Mr. West's old Krav Maga classroom—it was a semester after his death, and they still hadn't taken his name off the door—and took a breath. Four minutes late. I opened the door and slipped into line.

"Detention, Ms. Farina," Ms. King said from the head of the class.

Vera Hunt, the Prefect who was leading the beginning of class stretches, shook her head with exasperated amusement. Her surface thoughts drifted outside her mind like colorful, lazy clouds. *If this keeps up, Crystal will be here two weeks after everyone else gets out for the end of the year.*

I concealed a grin. "Yes, Ms. King."

I changed positions with the rest of the class. It was hard to believe that these stretches had once left me in a puddle on the floor. Now they were second nature. Most of it was Neal Black's training—he'd pushed me beyond my limits, watched me puke, then told me to get off the ground and try it again. If not for that, I probably wouldn't have survived a full semester here; let alone a full semester with secret meetings, trainings, and missions on top of my full school load. The only reason I had any free time to myself was because my blue lines let me keep up in academic classes. All the time that was supposed to be for homework had turned into design time for my inventions in R&D. Ms. King had appropriated both my Fridays and Saturdays to go over everything I should have learned before I was assigned to Tactical Team 47, which meant that the only day I had to myself was Sunday, when I finally got to go home.

It wasn't all bad. I could almost hold my own in hand-to-hand against Black, and the newer engineers in R&D spent so much time ogling at my work that it was easy to forget that ninety-eight percent of them had college degrees. Already, I was consulting with a team tasked with creating a new line of energy weapons equipped with limiters that restricted the electrical pulse—turning the device into a stunner. The designs were still preliminary, but working with that team had given me the idea to combine some of their basic membrane technology with my pulser to create a sort of energy shielding module. It was the opposite of an energy weapon—and much more my speed. Unfortunately, processing space was at a premium, so I'd only just started on the calculations. There was no sense in adding a processing-headache to the mix when I was only getting four hours of sleep a night.

I jotted down a quick mental note as another idea occurred to me. Perhaps I could persuade Ms. King to give me extra credit for my new developments in R&D. I couldn't ask now—applying for extra credit immediately after getting detention would probably make me lose points in class because it wasn't strategic. Of course, if I could engineer a situation to apply more of the things I'd learned in Social History while I asked about it, then I might get double the extra credit. Ms. King liked it when we tried to incorporate the manipulation techniques into our everyday lives.

I watched Ms. King out of the corner of my vision as she paced up and down the rows of students with a critical gaze. It was amazing how far she'd helped me come. I'd shown up on Martial Academy's doorstep terrified, clueless, and with abilities I didn't understand. Now, I was one of five projector telepaths on base, and fully capable of protecting myself.

She wasn't the only one who had helped me through my first semester. Thanks to Vera Hunt, memories of Zach were few and far between. I was more in control of myself than I'd ever been. I was tired, too, but it was a wonderful kind of tired.

I concealed a yawn as Hunt finished leading the stretches and dismissed us to grab a drink of water.

Perhaps I could ask them to delay the next briefing a bit. Fifteen extra minutes of sleep would go a long way—but it would also mean I was late to class more often. Today there had been a twenty minute buffer zone between when the briefing was supposed to end, and when class was supposed to start. Tolden hadn't let us go until three minutes before I was supposed to be in class. Even running, I had only made the rotunda before the gong rang.

Suddenly, Hunt stiffened. Her surface thoughts pulled back behind her walls, until they were well guarded enough that it would take some effort to break through.

"Uh, Ma'am?" she hurried up to Ms. King. Their voices

were low enough that only someone like Tabitha Smith—Tac 47's Auditory Analyst—would have been able to hear them. I merely detailed a few of my blue lines to watch their faces and translate what they were saying into text I could read off of my vision. That was one skill I'd developed in the Social History class. As long as I could see their faces, I could read their lips.

"Something just came up. I need to go." Hunt said.

Ms. King's eyes narrowed. "Fine."

Hunt hurried out.

Ms. King paired everyone up and demonstrated the first drill. Soon we were all breathing hard again. As I worked, I wondered what Hunt had left to do. She had remarkable control over her surface thoughts, to be able to shield them like that. While her walls weren't much of an obstacle for someone with my projection strength, it was impolite to drill inside someone's mind. Ms. King had been quite clear on that fact.

I wondered, for a moment, if Hunt knew about the Agency. She'd been at Martial Academy for four years, and she was observant. She had to have noticed something—though she might not have pursued it. I'd never seen her around the Agency's compound, and no one in Social History had ever mentioned her.

I pulled up an image of Hunt handing Mr. West a letter on the first day of school, last semester. Could she be working with the Company? That was one explanation, but it could have just as easily been a note about something else. She was a Prefect, after all. There were plenty of things non-Company related that could have been in that note. Short of asking, I really had no way to know.

The way Ms. King had let her go without asking any questions—verbal questions, anyway—made it seem like Hunt was working with the Agency but, if that was the case, why hadn't I heard about it? She'd been helping Ms. King teach Mr. West's class for a few weeks and, before that, she'd been teaching Ms. King's advanced classes. That meant Ms. King had to trust her, right? If Hunt was working for the Company, why would Ms. King be using her as an assistant teacher?

Or, maybe what Hunt was doing to help Ms. King didn't require much trust. It wasn't like Advanced Krav Maga was Social History, the class Ms. King used to vet new Agency recruits. Ms. King had mentioned something before about keeping enemies in sight and busy so they didn't do anything unexpected. This could be one of those cases.

::Farina, keep your mind on the fight,:: Ms. King snapped. I jerked my thoughts back to the present and managed to keep moving with the lines weaving around my vision. We were non-contact sparring, which didn't require much attention. I could tell my partner's intentions before he moved, so there was plenty of time to move out of the way and counterstrike. Unfortunately, Ms. King was the only person I'd met with a high enough PS rating to read my mind. Her touch was gentle, so I didn't usually notice it until she projected something to me.

::You can't always count on reading your opponent's mind to mean you are fast enough.::

She called a halt and moved partners around so I was paired with Briggs. He was with Mr. Mccoy's military group—recruited almost the moment he set foot on campus. He was good, but still not nearly as fast as Houston had been. When I was focused, keeping pace with him was easy. When I was distracted, I started lagging behind, which was no-doubt Ms. King's intention. I couldn't be sure if she knew that the two of us were friends. We'd met on my first day of school at Martial Academy when he and Tabitha Smith invited me to sit with them at lunch. Regardless, Briggs didn't slow down for anyone; not even a friend.

I refocused on Briggs, and made note of how he moved. His strength and speed were improving at a fantastic pace—his strength slightly more than his speed. It was probably due to all his extra weekend assignments with the military. I wasn't sure what sort of ringer Mr. Mccoy was putting his class through, but it must have been similar to what Black was doing with me. I was glad, though. Briggs was one of my friends here. He and Tabitha Smith were the first people to reach out and be friendly with me.

Five minutes before the gong rang, Ms. King froze. The door opened to show a larger woman with black hair like mine, cut at her chin. She scanned the room as she stepped inside with Hunt on her heels. Hunt's eyes were wider than usual, and a touch of anxiety hovered outside her walls. She took a deep breath as she came all the way into the room, and the anxiety disappeared. She was as calm and collected as ever.

I signalled to Briggs to stop the exercise and watched the newcomer carefully. Around me, the other drills slowed to a halt. The newcomer was scanning the room, so I took the opportunity to brush up against her mind. My eyes widened as I realized what she was doing—sorting us into groups. Ms. King and I went into the Beta-One category, while Hunt, and some of the less timid newbies, went into the Alpha-Niner category. I took note of those with a frown. If this woman knew about Neurodivergents, she would know that Ms. King, at least, was a Projector Telepath. Why sort her people into groups without taking precautions to shield her surface thoughts?

I examined her walls. They wouldn't be difficult to get through. The frequency shifted a lot, but the range was relatively small, and even the highest frequencies were set at half my capacity. If this newcomer was a telepath, I would eat my tactical suit.

She finished her inventory, then wrenched those thoughts back inside her walls. Her eyes locked on Ms. King, and she began to advance. Her thoughts whipped into a frenzy of accusation and hurt, only partially covered by a weak attempt at oozing false congeniality. She stopped inside Ms. King's personal space, and looked up at her with bared teeth. "I understand you've been substituting my class while I made arrangements to relocate here. Your services are no longer required."

Ms. King nodded and draped the room in soothing thoughts to try and calm the woman down, but it only enraged the storm of half-formed accusations whipping around the new teacher's mind.

Ms. King gestured to the students watching all around them. "Of course, anytime. I have a capable student instructor, so I would be more than happy to continue to assist you while you're settling in."

I tried to dive inside the new teacher's surface thoughts to see if I could find a single coherent word inside the storm, but the hatred clawed at my mind. These weren't just surface thoughts, these were raw emotions with such a low frequency that the newcomer couldn't shield them if she tried. Stepping inside would be like standing in front of a speeding semi truck.

The newcomer's eyes narrowed. "No, that won't be necessary. I understand that Ms. Hunt is here as my teacher aide today. Plus, it would be far below your pay grade, don't you think?"

Pay grade? It was a well known fact inside the Agency— and, apparently the Company, too—that Ms. King was the second most powerful person in the Agency's hierarchy. The only one with more clout was Ms. Green, the Agency's Director and the Administrator of Martial Academy. I concealed a smile. Both of them knew who the other worked for. If there hadn't been students here, this encounter might have left them both with some nasty bruises. Then I caught images drifting from the new teacher's thoughts and revised my estimation. If this had happened anywhere but this classroom, then one of them would be dead.

::Yes, my thoughts as well,:: Ms. King projected to me. ::You may not want to spend any time alone with her until she learns to control her hate. She is a powerful telekinetic—much more powerful than Houston—and she would be rated as far more dangerous if our analysts knew she was incapable of controlling herself. Once I've made my report, her danger rating will be revised.::

I nodded and Ms. King excused herself—leaving the rest of us with the new teacher, who introduced herself as Ms. Graff.

The rest of the week, classes with Elaine Graff were...interesting. She was aware that I could read her mind and solved the problem by making me her personal go-for. If I wasn't in the room, I couldn't cause problems for her and the Company. I couldn't tell whether she was amused at that fact, or exasperated by it. She could only come up with so many errands before what she was trying to do became obvious. When she couldn't find an excuse to keep me out of the room, she paired me with Hunt. I soon learned that Vera Hunt was a moderately powerful telekinetic—with instructions to use her abilities to compensate for mine. When I tried to put my brain on autopilot and direct my attention elsewhere, I ended up with my face on the mat and bruised ribs. She was always careful to make sure I didn't actually get hurt, but she didn't feel badly about it either. Her surface thoughts revealed that she really was doing her best to help me with my combat skills. As part of the Agency, I was going to need them.

I couldn't help but wonder how long Hunt had known I was working for the Agency. Would she have helped me those first few days of school if she had known I would be recruited by Ms. King? She had certainly become more distant after I was recruited. I had attributed it to the fact that I knew my way around the school now. I didn't need her help to figure out where I was supposed to go, but what if it was because she couldn't risk me accidentally reading her mind? She didn't seem to be that concerned about it while we were sparring, though. From what I could tell, she was genuinely focused on helping me improve my combat skills—and that meant knocking me on my butt every opportunity she could get.

I didn't dare complain. Ms. King would only use it as an illustration of what happened when I didn't keep my mind on the fight. After all, these were the people I had to learn to police. If a junior telekinetic could cause this many problems, what would happen when I did battle with an experienced one? What would happen when I came against a telepath more powerful than I was?

It was a possibility I didn't want to spend a lot of time on. After all, I wasn't on Tactical Team 47 as a Hitter. My job was to play comms, analyze data, and use my projection abilities to convince people to surrender without violence. Hurting people still turned my stomach.

At the end of the week, I was bruised, exhausted, and frustrated. This was the teacher the Company had sent to replace Earl West?

An image of his face—carefully blank as always—flashed through my head. He had worked for the Company, so the rest of my team dismissed his death as a tragic occurrence and left it at that. Every time I walked through Martial Academy's halls, I couldn't help but miss him. He had come to mean a lot to me in a short amount of time. While he hadn't always been forthcoming with information, he had always given sound advice. I missed that. Now he was being replaced by this naturally angry woman determined to keep me bruised on the mat or out of the room. She wasn't teaching, she was punishing.

CHAPTER TWO

I didn't say much during dinner with Briggs and Smith—which wasn't that strange. Smith kept up enough conversation to cover and, by the end of the meal, I had decided to skip tonight's Tournament. I'd gone every other day that week, which meant I could afford to miss. Maybe I would be able to catch up on some of my calculations—or maybe even some sleep. By the time the bell signalling our twenty minutes of homework rang, I had mustered some energy. Every bone in my body still groaned when I shifted, but I was going to have a whole hour to myself tonight, and that had to count for something.

Briggs pulled me aside as I reached the dining room door, though, and I let him. He glanced at the motley of bruises that covered my arm from shoulder to wrist. "Is there something else going on here that I don't know about?"

I froze; my thoughts racing. Had Briggs picked up on the fact that there were a lot of neurodivergents in this school? I scanned his surface thoughts and relaxed fractionally. His mind was full of concern about how hard Ms. Graff and Vera Hunt were pushing me in class—and my ability to handle the pressure.

I bit my lip as I tried to decide how to handle this. I certainly couldn't tell him that the reason I was getting hit so hard was because Ms. Graff hated my guts, and was taking every opportunity to make me regret being in her class. Then I would have to explain why this teacher I'd only met a few days ago hated me so much—and I'd have to do it without mentioning the Agency.

Finally, I forced a smile. "It's just how these things work, right? I've got to get better so I can defend myself."

Briggs shook his head. "Crystal, this isn't normal. I see how Ms. Graff looks at you, and she isn't happy. You can't take a whole semester of this."

My smile softened just a bit. Briggs had no idea what I could handle. These bruises were painless, next to some of the injuries I'd had over the years. If I had to deal with Ms. Graff for a whole semester, I would bear it with a smile. Her training wasn't half as bad as my sessions with Black—at least Hunt tried to pull her punches. At the end of the day, more of the bruises were probably from Black than Hunt. I couldn't exactly tell Briggs that, though. There was no way I could explain away a private hand-to-hand instructor working with me during the time I was *supposed* to be in detention.

"I'll be fine, Briggs. Thanks for the concern."

I started to turn away, but Briggs grabbed my hand. "Look, I know you think you can take care of yourself, but I've been watching you fight. I think I can help."

I arched my eyebrows. I had at least four people trying to "help" me with my hand-to-hand, and the result was the bruises he saw. One more person wasn't going to do much— but Briggs's eyes were so earnest, I wanted to give him a chance. He really did want to help me, and he was convinced he could.

"What's your idea?" I asked, finally. Seeing what he had to say couldn't hurt.

Brigg moved so he was standing in front of me, his eyes suddenly alight with excitement. "You've got the same problem I had as a kid."

My eyes widened as I picked up some of his surface thoughts. He was remembering flashes of the training his family had put him through. I caught glimpses of him, barely knee high, dressed in the white Gi I saw some of the students at Martial Academy wearing. It was required for some Asian styles, although Krav Maga only required unrestrictive clothing. Briggs's emotions around that time were complicated, but mostly overrun with frustration as his parents corrected him time and time again.

I suppressed the urge to shake my head as I freed myself from his surface thoughts. Briggs had been fighting since he was a kid, and he was in the beginning Krav Maga class with me? Why?

Briggs must have seen some of my questions on my face, because he laughed. "Yeah, I know, right? My whole family does martial arts. I was practically raised in a dojo, but we do Okinawan styles at home. Israeli military hand-to-hand is crazy different, so I'm in the beginning class. But it doesn't matter what style you're working in. Unless you learn to commit, you're never going to get anywhere."

I pressed my lips together. "I commit when I need to."

Briggs shook his head. "That's not going to be good enough. Part of practicing martial arts is practicing the will to defend yourself. Commitment is a skill, not just a decision. That's one of the reasons Kata work is so important in the styles I grew up in. Katas aren't just for practicing how to string all the moves together, it's for practicing the will to defend yourself. It doesn't matter how good your technique is. If it takes a conscious decision to potentially kill someone else in order to defend yourself, those crucial seconds may cost you your life."

I swallowed as I felt his conflicted emotions rising back to the surface of his thoughts. The decision to potentially kill someone in defense wasn't any easier for him than it was for me. Unlike Black, he understood exactly how much it would cost.

He was right about how it was impacting me, though. I spent extra seconds weighing the cost of every violent action before I committed. I scanned every force reading, and plotted every motion exactly. I waited for my blue lines instead of acting on instinct. If the blue lines showed that I had a significant chance of killing the other person, I changed tactics and then waited for the new evaluation. In a word, I was slow. Sure, I was much faster than most of the newbies who still had to think through all the in-between steps of every single technique, but when it really came down to it, I wouldn't be fast enough. For now, I could get away with handicapping myself by avoiding death blows. Later, though? I was going to have to decide what was more important: keeping my hands clean, or staying alive.

Briggs clapped a hand on my shoulder. "Hey, you ever want to talk about it, let me know, yeah? It's hard to practice like you're in the real deal, but it should keep the new teacher off your back. It'll help you be faster against Hunt, anyway."

I mustered a smile for him. "Thanks."

He shrugged. "I only ever had my mom railing on me about it. I can't imagine how hard it is having the teacher *and* Hunt on your case. Hunt can be scary when she gets passionate about things. My big brother was a year ahead of her, so I've heard all sorts of stories. There's a reason she's not allowed to register for Tournament anymore."

"Wait, she's not *allowed*? I thought Prefects were encouraged to participate in Tournament."

Briggs shook his head. "Hunt seems scary outside of the ring, but she changes when she fights. If ever there's someone who understands commitment, it's her. You saw her last year with—what was his name again?" He waved a hand and started walking down the hall. I followed him. "Anyway, she's not just like that when she's trying to teach dirtbags a lesson. When she fights, she fights until the other guy's crippled or dead. She takes zero chances. And, while she might be a little bit excessive, she is also the last person anyone would ever want to pick a fight with."

We kept walking until we reached the end of the hallway. Briggs waved. "Just think about it, yeah?"

I forced myself to grin. "Thanks, Briggs." He entered his dorm room, and I entered mine. As much as I didn't want to admit it, Briggs did have a point. One of these days, I was going to fight someone who was faster and stronger than I was. If I was still pulling my punches for fear of accidentally killing someone, I wouldn't survive the encounter. The best way to prepare for that was to practice committing to a fight, now.

I picked up my homework, and started writing down the pre-computed answers I pulled from the archives of my mind. Briggs really was a true friend. Even though he had no clue what was going on at this school, he was still trying to help. I couldn't stop my grin as I re-focused on my homework. I really was so lucky to be surrounded by such caring people.

The next night, Tolden sent me home early from the team exercises with strict instructions to get some rest, then be back early on Saturday, and I was too tired to argue. I took the subway home, and spent most of that time trying to clear the backlog of calculations I needed for my new electric version of the plasma pulser.

I opened the door to find Mom sitting on the counter with her eyes glued to the door again. She didn't respond when I shut the door gently behind me—even though she was staring right through me. She was too busy muttering things under her breath. My blue lines started decoding them as I approached.

"I don't want you to. I can push through it—I know I can. I won't endanger the team again."

"What team?" I asked.

She gasped and looked up. Her eyes snapped back to the present. I felt a spike of fear in her surface thoughts, and then it disintegrated. Ashes of fear swirled around her mind. "Where have you been? And don't tell me you had to walk your friend home." She stopped and sought my eyes. For once, I let her and then gasped as the world around me faded.

Everything except my pounding heartbeat vanished. There was nothing but her green eyes and pain. Pain of loss. Pain of betrayal. The feeling of fire burning her skin—

I tried to look away to break the connection, but there was flame everywhere I looked. I pounded at the confines of her mind, but they were impenetrable like iron. I turned as another mind brushed mine. It was hungry—desperate for release, and willing to do anything to escape. I spun my senses around, questing for the origin of that terrifying mind, but it was nowhere to be found.

The walls grew hot behind me and I jerked away. Smoke stung my eyes, my throat. I gasped for air, but I couldn't breathe! I choked, and staggered back toward the safety of my own mind. Flame sprung up to block my path everywhere I turned. There was no escape.

::Help!:: The cry was met with silence as blackness started flickering at the edge of my vision.

This was why I didn't meet people's eyes. This was why I never looked higher than the floor.

A few months of camaraderie had made me stupid. I had abandoned my sense of caution. I knew eyes had claws. I knew I could get trapped!

As darkness folded in on my vision I felt a cool, gentle touch amidst the flames. ::You shouldn't come here, child. You aren't strong enough yet.::

I knew that voice—strong, and feminine—from sometime before Dad left. Sometime—

The thought was gone, wiped away by a gentle hand. That

same hand pushed me, and suddenly I was flying.

I stumbled back and caught myself against the wall, trembling, and safe in my own mind once more. The surface was cool and reassuring. It reminded me that I was securely inside my own mind. I pulled my braided hair over my shoulder, and leaned my head against the wall. This solid, constant pressure was what safety felt like.

Mom crossed the room and took my hand. "Are you alright?"

I looked back at her, careful to keep my mind in my own head. How could she have not felt that? Something inside her head was burning. It had snatched me away from my own mind and tried to set me on fire, too. Could she really just ignore that?

But if she couldn't feel the burning in her own mind, I wasn't going to draw any attention to it. Mom was strange, kind of like me. Her mind was different—which was how she knew how to help me build the blue lines I used to function in day-to-day life. Maybe those differences protected her from that burning monster. If I tampered without more information, I could cause some huge problems for her.

"I'm fine," I lied, and pulled my hand away. "How was your day?"

She looked at the clock, and then back at me. "I'm sure it was fine. To be honest, I don't remember much."

I bit my lip. Maybe she had been trapped inside whatever that was too. Was that why she had those fits? She forgot a lot of things. Perhaps she also forgot the burning monster inside her mind?

I added it to my list of things to ask someone at the Agency.

"Remember to take your medication tonight, Mom," I said. The medications her psychiatrist, Dr. Carlisle, prescribed helped when she got this bad. She didn't always like to take them and I could understand why. I never took any of the meds Dr. Carlisle prescribed either. They made it harder to think, like my blue lines were weighted down by something. The difference was that I wasn't haunted by burning monsters in my mind.

She nodded and started to drift away, only to stop. She was staring at the couch in front of the TV, blinking. "When did that come?"

The dilapidated couch that had been bled on so many times before, first by me during my time with Zach, then by Tabitha Smith last semester, was gone—replaced by a tope, faux leather, overstuffed beauty.

"You didn't order it?" I asked. It was possible that she'd seen how the old one was falling apart, ordered a new one, and then completely forgotten about it. That was unlikely, given that Mom would have had to notice that the old couch needed to be replaced.

Mom shook her head. She stared at it for another long moment, and then her eyes glazed over and she started to wander off again.

"Mom, wait."

She turned slowly, with a dreamy smile on her face to complement her thin bones and pallid skin.

"Are you sure you're alright?" I asked.

Her smile faded. "You're stronger than you were before, Crystal. You remind me of—" A spasm ran through her body, snapping her mouth and eyes closed.

"Mom!" I was only halfway across the room before her eyes opened again, and the corners of her mouth turned up.

"Nevermind," she said with a wave. She turned to go back into her bedroom.

I let my shields down to try and brush her mind, then stopped as I remembered the fire. What if I got trapped again? But Mom really wasn't alright. Every day, she was getting worse. I wondered if I should try to find another doctor to help, but brushed that thought off as soon as I had it. She'd already been to all the doctors in Chicago, and none of them had a clue. Doctors couldn't help Mom.

"Who do I remind you of?" I asked, instead.

She didn't turn to look at me, only shook her head. "I don't remember. It was a long, long time ago. Too long to make any difference. Just be careful, Crystal. You never know what monsters lurk in the night, and no one is strong enough to hold them all off."

I shuddered inside, but let her go.

Instead, I turned my attention to the mysterious couch. Upon close observation, the piece of furniture was new. It smelled of factory dyes and, faintly, of perfume. There were two sets of gloved handprints on either armrest from where it had been carried inside, still perfectly undisturbed. It had to have been moved within the last few hours, then, because Mom hadn't been home from work for very long and she often sat and watched television before making dinner.

Whoever had brought it inside knew Mom's work schedule. I pulled the cushions off, and analyzed the underside for any sign that they'd stored something nefarious inside—but there was nothing. Only a little note concealed as the tag on the underside. If this was a Trojan horse, it had been built for that purpose from the ground up. I gripped the tag between my fingers and scanned its contents.

Apparently Ms. King had heard that Agent Smith had bled all over the last one. The Agency wanted to replace it. The couch was a reward for helping Tabitha last semester after Doug Houston had discovered that she was keeping tabs on him. He'd beat her up twice, consecutively, and might have even killed her if I hadn't shown up. At the time, I hadn't known anything about neurodivergents or Psionics. All I knew was that Tabitha had been friendly to me, and that she was hurt. I had never expected the Agency to compensate me for those actions any more than they'd already done. Ms. King had allowed me to receive my permanent Biocard—a piece of technology implanted in my head that boosted my Psionic abilities—far sooner than most recruits, and placed me on Tactical Team 47. She'd given me a home, and that was recompense enough.

I sat back, considering the gift for a long time. I pulled the memory of Tabitha Smith laying on the old couch, and the pinprick of blood she'd left behind. It certainly was less noticeable than some of the bloodstains I'd gotten out of it before; so why bother? The only answer I could find was that this was a gift of thanks from Ms. King. I had saved her student's life, and she wanted me to know that she appreciated it.

Carefully, I detached the tag from the inside of the couch, then shredded it. Ms. King had been clear on that, at least. Any written communications from the Agency were to be destroyed as soon as they were read. I wasn't sure if this counted as being directly from the Agency, but it did mention Agent Smith. I put the pieces of the tag on a plate and lit them on fire. A moment later, they were curled, charred slag I could throw in the trash.

After I cleaned the plate I'd used to burn the message, I glued a few pieces of bread together with peanut butter and jam. It was a sorry excuse for dinner, but I was exhausted. I put one sandwich in Mom's hands, then watched to make sure she ate it. When she was done, I watched her take her medication, then tucked her into bed. She dozed off almost immediately.

In spite of my exhaustion, I laid in bed for a long time,

staring at the spartan walls and ceiling. Part of me wondered what I would say when Mom inevitably asked about the couch again. How many times had I lied in the last week? How many more times would I have to lie to cover the fact that I was never home? Mom was going to get worried if I didn't have some sort of excuse for being on base all the time—but I had a job to do. I had people to protect.

I rolled onto my side and clutched the blankets closer.

Part of me wondered why I had to lie. Wouldn't it be better to let her in on this new world? But then I saw her pallid skin and gaunt cheeks in my mind. She didn't need anything else to worry about—especially not me.

I was going to have to ask Tolden for more time off, though. When Mom got this bad, sometimes she had accidents. I would need to check in on her as often as I could. Maybe I could convince someone from Tac 47 to drive me home for a few minutes at the end of every school day.

I started running some probabilities as I had another thought. If I could see something inside Mom's head burning, then maybe someone at the Agency would be able to help her. Maybe doctors couldn't figure out what was going on with Mom because it was a Psionic issue?

My blue lines ran into some snags, calculating the percentages, but I drove them through those rough patches. These numbers were important. If someone at the Agency could help Mom, I would do anything I had to in order to heal her mind.

The blue lines blinked an answer in front of my eyes as they finally spit out their numbers.

Ninety-seven percent chance of death. Three percent unknown. If I told anyone in the Agency about Mom's burning mind, she would die.

I hissed. How was that possible? I pulled the underlying

data to do a more intentional analysis, but the data was gone. All that remained was a phrase I never remembered writing.

"If you want Adalind to stay alive, keep her away from all this. The Agency can never know about her."

I twisted the plasma pulser ring on my finger like it would lend me some vestige of comfort. It was just cold.

Where had that message come from? It was written into the lining of my mind like it belonged there.

Regardless, I couldn't drag Mom into this mess. I would ask around discreetly, to see if I could find something that could help her, but I couldn't tell Mom about any of this until I knew more about what was going on with her.

CHAPTER THREE

The next morning, I made Mom some breakfast and left it on the counter for her to find when she woke up, along with a note about having forgotten something at school. I made it to school fifteen minutes early, and found Ms. King and Tabitha Smith standing by the entrance to the elevator in the back of her classroom with long fabric draped over her arm. Any questions I'd been planning to ask about Mom—covertly, and without getting Mom involved—got pushed to the back of my mind as my blue lines converged on the fabric Ms. King held. A quick analysis showed that it was a blood red dress—a complement to the blue one Tabitha was wearing. It was floor length, and rippled with every motion Tabitha made, from the beaded top, to the floor.

Abnormal conditions noted flashed on my vision. The way the bottom of the skirt amplified any motion from the bodice indicated that it couldn't possibly be normal fabric. The sheen coming off the beads was only a sixty-point-two percent match to the beads I'd seen on clothing. What was it?

Ms. King chuckled as she noted my confusion. "That's the same look Tabitha got when she heard the rustle of the fabric—or lack of it, anyway."

"Something that moves this much should be loud. These sounds have been damped." Tabitha smoothed the sides of the dress down.

"That's because it's not fabric," someone else said. The elevator doors opened to reveal Cal, the head of R&D. I'd worked with her intermittently on projects when I needed a second opinion. More often than that, I helped her track down Steele when he was dodging her calls. Apparently he felt the same way about physical engineering as I felt about software engineering.

She glanced at Tabitha. "It is gorgeous on you, though. I had worried about the height modifications, but it looks to be working better than the last round, don't you agree?"

The engineer's declaration that the dress was not made of fabric prompted a second round of analysis. I still couldn't come up with a name for the polymer, but the function was clear. "It absorbs energy."

"Right!" Cal snapped her fingers at me, and spun. "That thing will stop a bullet, slow a knife, and let you walk away more-or-less intact if you get hit by a truck—so long as it hits the dress, and not the sleeves."

"What sleeves?" Tabitha beat me to the question. The dress had a high neckline with no sleeves. The effect was a beautiful piece of bulletproof art to wear at a party, with a glaring weak point.

Cal laughed. "Exactly. Now let's get back down to nerd town, and I'll get started with the *real* briefing."

Ms. King handed me the red dress. "I'll be back in a few hours to give you your assignment. Until then, work with Cal. She's got experience few people still working here do."

I looked at the slip of not-fabric in my hands, then looked back up at Cal. What, exactly, was I supposed to do with this? Work out the math?

"There's a place to change in R&D. Don't worry, it's not as frivolous as it looks—and you're in Tac Block 4, which means you're just as likely as Medina's people to actually use the thing." Cal's intent was clear. I was going to have to put it on.

I followed Cal into the elevator, racking my memory for the last time I'd actually worn a dress—and the only times I could come up with were parties where Zach had made me wear this little black slip of fabric he called a dress. In the six months we dated, it happened three times. Before that, nothing. It was hard not to look at the dress in my hand with disgust.

"Hey, I get it!" Cal said as we exited the elevator and made our way across the rotunda that served as the heart of the Agency. "I wasn't really one for dresses, either. They tend to get caught in gears, or stained with motor oil, or torn, or melted—I could go on. But every once in a while, a girl likes to look good. The fact that you're bulletproof—"

"—except for the arms," Tabitha interjected.

"—is just a plus. And anyway, you're going to end up in places where formal attire is absolutely required in order to do your job. What if there was a telekinetic assassin determined to assassinate the British Prime Minister while she was at a party? Are you going to walk in *there* with a tactical suit? Imagine what a stir that would create!"

"It's the formal version of our tactical suit," Tabitha said. "There's not quite as much storage in the girl's version, but Tolden and the others can keep all the tactical suit toys in their tuxedos. We've got to learn to improvise a bit. Also, fashion has officially taken precedence over safety." She glared at her bare arms for emphasis. "First, no pants pockets in street clothes, then no arm protection in battle dresses. What's next? Are you going to take the spikes out of our heels?"

Spikes in our heels? I inspected a few images from when I'd seen stilettos in stores. The shoes themselves were spikes. Had R&D modified them even farther? I could see the appeal of a last-ditch knife hidden in the heel, but it was no substitute to a gun on my belt. "We have room for our firearms still, right?" I asked. If I was wearing something like Tabitha was, I wanted as many weapons as I could get.

Cal swiped us into a room just down the hallway from the makespace where I usually worked before she answered. "Depends on the type. You have to leave the heavy stuff, but you can definitely still fit a glock. I'm sure we could even modify the dress to carry a power pack for that plasma pulser of yours—and we definitely could for the electric one you're working on. You want a rifle, you're out of luck."

Which didn't disqualify any of my weaponry. Black hadn't cleared me with anything larger than a handgun yet—although I'd proved my mettle with every weapon we'd tried so far.

"I'll get started with Agent Smith out here, while you go change." Cal said, and motioned to another door at the side of the room, just to the right of a two lane shooting range. I hurried to do as I was asked.

The dress fit snugly around my body. The beaded top was stiff like armor, but I could still feel the breeze generated around my waist by the skirt. The tactile input was strange—I rolled it around in my mind for a moment, and then decided I didn't like it. It took too much processing away from what was around me to deal with the fact that I felt naked from the waist down.

In the mirror, I didn't look like me. My black hair was still in a ponytail, and my eyes were still green. Everything else was wrong. The dress cupped my breasts, leaving nothing to the imagination, and then nipped in to my waist which was small, but muscled. I could see the curve of my hips and how it tapered down to meet my long legs, like in one of those magazines at the store. This was the farthest thing from the baggy blue jeans and black hoodie I wore to insulate myself from searching stares while I was on the street. I looked weak like one of those models—fake, like I was pretending for Zach.

I pushed the images of him firmly away and took a deep breath. Zach was gone. I hadn't thought of him in half a semester, and I wasn't going to start now. I was a tactical agent, not his plaything, and this was so I could do a job. In Social History, they talked about the importance of deception. This was just an illusion. Just because I looked weak, didn't mean I was. Just because this dress made my arms look small and easily snapped didn't mean I couldn't hold my own in a fight. I let them see the curve of my hips so they would be distracted, and then I could take anything I needed to take. It was a game.

That didn't mean I had to like it, or that I felt any less naked.

I took a deep breath, then froze as air skated up and down my legs. The hem of the dress flipped out and then back to try and spread the motion over as much surface area as possible—distributing the force and decreasing the pressure.

I pushed the calculations away and nodded at myself in the mirror. I could do this—

The bob of my head set the dress dancing again, and another set of numbers rose to my vision. I bit my lip. This was going to be annoying.

Cal gasped when I finally got the courage to come out of the changing room. "I knew you would look good, 32, but you're absolutely stunning! You should dress up more often."

I clenched my teeth. "Let's just get this done as quickly as we can. It's driving me crazy!" Suddenly feeling naked wasn't nearly as much of a problem. I didn't have time to focus on that because every time I shifted, the dress sent changing patterns of air against my legs, and another round of analysis started. I could shut it down, but that took effort. I could already see the headache that would come if I had to stay like this for over an hour.

"What's the problem?" she asked, suddenly concerned.

"The airwaves. Even breathing sends airwaves everywhere!"

Cal was already nodding. "You have some tactile sensory issues, and this is very different, isn't it? One moment."

She disappeared for an eternity, then returned with some new slips of fabric. "It's the same stuff we use to line all of

Black's clothes—he's got a similar problem, you know. I can redo the lining of the bodice later to try and minimize some of the issues, but we can start by putting these leggings on. It should feel more like you're wearing pants."

Sure enough, the leggings she'd given me calmed the storm of analysis. The dress was bearable. It was still fake and uncomfortably skin tight, but I could deal with discomfort now that the sensory overload was gone.

Cal grinned. "See? Not so bad now. I'll add your name to the tactile lists in our tailoring section to prevent more mishaps like this down the road—and you tell us if there's anything you want modified. That's one thing about a place where everyone's neurodivergent. Everyone's got their quirks, and not everyone's equipped to communicate them, so we learn to watch for things like this. In engineering, we try to tailor everything so that it works for the individual agents. The last thing you need is to be fighting sensory overload while you're in the field."

Cal guided me over to where Tabitha was checking the equipment she'd stowed in her dress, and showed me how to secure the leg harnesses that would hold whatever equipment I'd picked for the mission. The dress had a slit I could activate by pressing a certain spot in the beading on the bodice of the dress. In the current configuration, the slit only stayed open for two seconds before it tried to re-fuse—to prevent anyone from noting the gun I had strapped to the inside of my leg. It took a few tries before I could retrieve any of the items I'd stowed within the two second window without accidentally getting my hand caught in the fabric.

"A few more days of practice, and you'll be almost as good at retrieval as Smith is," Cal said.

I looked at Tabitha, who was standing in the nearest shooting lane. Her hand moved like a blur as she pulled the weapon, sighted, and fired. The whole sequence only took one-point-six seconds.

"She's one of the fastest we've got. I thought Medina would snatch her up for the intelligence half of InDep, but she got assigned to Tactical 47 instead—due to her analysis skills, if I had to guess. Every team in Tac block 4 needs someone who's good at infiltration, and Smith's it."

Tabitha put her gun away again and turned. She probably heard the whole conversation. "I don't know how good I am, but it is fun," she said. Her voice was still quiet, and her eyes were still on the ground, but her head was lifted just enough for me to read the words on her lips.

Cal sighed. "It is, isn't it? One day, you're going to miss it."

Tabitha arched an eyebrow. "You used to work in InDep, right? Before you transferred to a post in R&D?"

"How did you guess that?" Cal asked, then waved a hand. "Nevermind, I should know better than to ask you analysis types. You're right, though. I started as a deep cover agent. After a while, it got too dangerous. I wanted something more stable, so I came here and started designing technology to help the agents I'd left in the field. One thing led to another, and I ended up as the head of R&D. That's how things tend to go here. They use you for what talents they need the most—doesn't matter if you're good at it by accident—until you can't do it anymore. Then you've got your pick of assignments."

Which was why I was working in TacDep instead of spending all my time in R&D with my motorcycle, or shielding module, or the grappling hook design I discovered in the archives of my mind last week. The Agency needed my analysis abilities to help Tac 47. They had plenty of people who could come up with innovative technology like the dress I was wearing.

Cal must have seen some of my thoughts on my face—that, or she was a telepath—because she said, "The sort of field work you'll be doing really isn't too hard. You use skills you're going to have to develop either way. As a projector telepath, your mind operates on a higher frequency than most, so you can get inside their heads to find the information you need. The biggest problem is that—for an intel extraction operation—you don't want them to know you're there. Many experienced Psionics can tell if a telepath is deep enough in their mind to search for information, so you'll be restricted to reading surface thoughts."

Tabitha smiled. "How horribly difficult. *Some* of us have to manipulate them into telling us what we need to know." Her surface thoughts revealed the sarcasm that must have been heavy in her voice, even though I couldn't decipher it. I took a moment to be grateful for my newfound telepathy. It made social situations so much simpler.

"The key is guiding the conversation so that they start actively thinking about the information you need without them knowing that's what you're after," Cal explained.

I got the sinking feeling she was about to try and teach me how to do exactly that.

Cal and Tabitha, who had evidently gone through this training before—understandable given that she'd been recruited by the Agency about a year before she transferred to Martial Academy—spent the next three hours, twenty-two minutes, and eight seconds trying to build on what Ms. King had taught the Social History class about the 'art of conversation'. When my brain started to hurt from absorbing those rules, they moved on to how to walk in a dress, and the unique tools the dress gave for distracting men. Most of it was just an extension of things Ms. King had already touched on in her Social History class, but it still made me feel like when I used to pretend for Zach. How could Tabitha stand this? All these lies and deceptions?

I was relieved when Black arrived to start the next section—

how to fight in a dress.

By the end of that session, I was certain the dress really was bulletproof. If it could survive completely unscathed from a sparring match with Black, it could survive anything. When Black finally conceded that I wouldn't trip over the dress in a fight, I reported back to Cal. Finally, I would be able to take the dress off—even if it was only for a few minutes while I ate lunch.

When I headed to the changing room to get in my street clothes again, Cal stopped me with a smile.

Instead of giving me a few minutes of respite, she sent me up to the Agency cafeteria with the blasted thing still on. Her surface thoughts revealed that she wanted me to get used to wearing it, but I was sure she was partially motivated by sheer cruelty. Still, lunch didn't last long, and most of the tactical agents in the cafeteria didn't stare. They'd probably had the same training. That reassuring fact didn't keep my ears from heating every time someone looked at me, though.

Tabitha didn't mind. It came a lot more naturally to her. She moved with the dress like she was born to it. Her conversation skills were great, too. I wondered if it was because, while I was busy analyzing colors and designing holographic models of the things I saw, Tabitha was busy doing the same with every conversation she heard.

"Tolden should have sent you down to talk to Houston," I said, during a break in the training. She might have been able to convince him to come in without a fight.

Tabitha frowned. "That might have been the plan. I've been slated to join Tac 47 for the better part of the year, and it isn't unknown for someone to be backed on their graduate assignment by their eventual team. Knowing what actually happened, though, I'm glad it wasn't me. Manipulating conversations is great when you don't know who you're talking to. Houston would have heard my lies almost immediately, and I probably wouldn't have survived."

I reviewed the conversation I'd had with Houston again and nodded. Tabitha was right. She might be better at conversation, but she didn't have my plasma pulser, and she couldn't have screamed in his mind to keep him from using his telekinesis—although maybe her telekinesis would have helped keep him from almost shooting Tolden. I wasn't entirely sure how a tug-of-war between telekinetics worked. I made a note to pay more attention to the telekinetics in Social History. That data might mean the difference between life and death one day.

The fight to bring Houston in still seemed like it happened yesterday—maybe last week. I could hardly believe it had been almost a full semester.

::Well believe it, Farina, and move on. You'll have plenty more missions like that before you're through.:: Ms. King's mind voice echoed in my head a moment before she strode through the door. She wore a floor length black dress that shimmered as she shifted. It didn't have the same wave pattern as Tabitha or my dress did—but it wasn't normal fabric, either. My lines started analysis without prompting, but came up empty. I archived that analysis branch and returned to the original evaluation of Ms. King. Her hair was done up behind her and studded with pearls. Her eyes were shadowed with makeup that accentuated her deep brown eyes, and there were heels on her feet that made her already tall form tower above me. Tabitha looked like a dwarf when she came over. I was just short.

I brushed off the incongruity of the situation. Me, feeling short? I was six feet tall!

"Oh, don't worry about it so much, Farina. I'll make sure you get some heels, too. The question is whether you'll be able to walk in them or not," Ms. King said.

"She can handle some kitten heels. We'll have to train her in the taller ones," Cal said.

I shrugged. "I'm just not used to being short."

"Well, all the girls at the fundraiser tonight will be in heels, too, so you'd better get used to the feeling. Come on, you're almost late for your hair appointment."

Tabitha grinned, and grabbed my hand. "Oh, he'll have a field day with your hair. I can't wait to see what he does with it!"

I stared at her dumbly. How could Tabitha be so excited about the smallest things? My hair? It was a thing to be cared for and kept out of the way. The only reason I hadn't cut it by now was because I didn't trust Mom with scissors, and we could hardly afford a hair appointment.

Maybe this new stylist person would cut it for me?

I dismissed that thought as I caught the picture of a man, brown hair close cropped around his ears, with unnaturally tailored eyebrows and a nose ring. He had a statistical resemblance to those models on the cover of magazines, too—once I'd reverse-engineered the image editing, anyway. Tabitha was right. He was going to love having access to so much long hair—which meant he was hardly going to solve my hair problem. Had I unwittingly wandered into a model agency?

I must have said at least part of that out loud, because both Tabitha and Cal laughed.

"Most of our agents can get by flaunting the rules of society. As long as they do their jobs, we don't care—in fact, we embrace it. We give them the training they need to communicate, help them when they fall short of that, and make sure they can succeed at their job. Agents on the Flex Tac block don't have that luxury. You need to understand how to act in all situations—whether you're at a bar, or a fundraiser for big donors. Fortunately, not all neurodivergents have mathematics specialties. Some actually perseverate on fashion-driven communication," Cal said.

Ms. King nodded. "Quite. Now come along, girls. Don't keep our stylist waiting."

The styling appointment proved to be far less intensive than the dress training had been. Mostly, he talked about proper hair and skin upkeep, made some recommendations on makeup, and showed me how to apply the basics. I sat in the chair and let him use his brushes, and sprays, and sparkles. When I finally got the chance to look at the mirror, I gasped. I wasn't Crystal anymore, I was someone else. Someone with long eyelashes that shielded narrow green eyes, proud arched eyebrows, and luxurious, shimmering hair that curled around my face and lengthened my neck. Powder dusted my skin all the way down to where it met the crimson top of the dress, smoothing my complexion and blending the colors with what he'd applied to my face. I sat taller, with a sultry look that contrasted sharply with the gun in my thigh holster. A quick analysis showed that he hadn't changed anything except the hair—but the optical illusion was enough.

I wasn't sure whether I should be happy or furious that they'd taken me and turned me into some rich princess.

"Don't worry, it's not permanent," Ms. King said. "But there are certain societal expectations when you go to a party like this. The first is that you fit in physically with the rest of the crowd."

Tabitha was bouncing in her chair with excitement. She knocked a strand of hair loose, and it fell over her eyes. The stylist rushed to fix it, and I got another lungfull of hairspray.

"What's our mission?" Tabitha asked when the air had cleared enough to breathe again.

Ms. King grinned. "Agent Smith, there are going to be a mix of individuals in attendance. I want you to figure out which of them work for—or with—us, and which work with the United States Armed Forces. If there are any other players there, you should make a note of it as well. Additionally, I would like a rough count of the Psionics present. Agent Farina, you need a little more practice with your compulsion. Figure out who is on the edge of donating more money than usual, and use your gifts to gently convince them to donate more. Martial Academy—and the Agency—can use all the funding we can get."

I thought about the assignment as we followed Ms. King back to the school. It felt kind of...dirty. Like I was going to be stealing. I understood that we were being trained to manipulate people, but making them give us money? Even if they were already planning on donating, it didn't feel right.

As we approached the dining room—where the fundraiser was being held—I stopped.

"Ms. King?" I asked. Ms. King turned to look at me. Her face was carefully neutral. "Can I have a different assignment?"

"Is there a problem with your current one?"

My cheeks started to burn. Ms. King obviously thought this dishonesty was worth it in the long run, or she wouldn't have given me the mission. This was my opportunity to prove that I understood her lessons. This was the application of my training.

But stealing? From donors? "I just don't think this is right. I know I'm just supposed to be nudging people into giving slightly more money than they were planning on giving—but these are Turnips, right? Aren't they the ones we're supposed to be protecting? Manipulating them just doesn't feel right."

Her eyes hardened, and she looked me over. "I see. Agent Smith, you can proceed with your assignment. Check back with me before you leave."

Tabitha left in a hurry, leaving me alone in the hallway with Ms. King. I could catch the trepidation wafting from her—quickly cleared away by the excitement of the upcoming mission.

"Agent Farina, you're refusing an assignment for moral reasons?" Ms. King's eyes seemed to drill into my skull.

I ducked my head. "Yes, Ma'am."

Her lips curled into an icy smile. "I thought you might."

Of all the things I had been expecting her to say, that wasn't one of them. I released a breath I didn't realize I'd been holding.

"I recruit students who I think may have gifts, whether it is analysis, Psionics, communication, combat—understand, the gifts are what get you in. What separates us from catch-all organizations like the Company is that we also require our recruits to have a strong moral compass. When I met you, I knew you would never take another human's life. You abhor violence, and that made you a prime candidate for the Agency."

I blinked. Had this been a test? The Agency recruited people with moral scruples, and Ms. King was checking to make sure I wouldn't abandon mine because a superior had told me to? That didn't seem very much like her. If I so much as revealed trepidation about doing something she'd asked, I would get a lecture on insubordination and the proper mindset for a student. If I was lucky, the lecture would stop there. Most of the time, she followed up her fifteen minute rant with an extra assignment to analyse command structures throughout history and then look at what happened when those command structures broke down.

Ms. King's smile disappeared. "That said, you are expected to air any concerns during a mission briefing. There are very few things that can get you ejected from the Agency. Insubordination—or refusing to do as a superior tells you—is one of those things, along with misusing your gift and fraternizing with other organizations who hold different goals to ours."

A chill ran down my spine. Did that mean—

"Now don't go jumping to any conclusions, Farina. Most recruits get all this information during their second year in the Social History course, after they've been vetted and accepted as a formal recruit. In some cases, like Agent Smith's, it is given during an external training course by their primary recruiter before they are funneled into my course. Your acceptance process was a little bit different, so you've been operating without that knowledge. That said, don't let this happen again. Speak up during the mission brief, or don't speak up at all."

I nodded. "Yes, Ma'am."

She sighed. "Now, what would you suggest I use as an alternative training mission?"

I thought for a moment. "Martial Academy gets anonymous donations, right? What if I give you a list of those who are donating, but don't want to be named?"

Ms. King thought for a moment, then nodded. "But I want a complete list. Understand? You'll have to talk to nearly everyone there. And Farina?" she met my gaze, projecting utmost seriousness. "They aren't all Turnips. Some of the people here were trained by the Agency, even though they now work in the private sector. They don't take kindly to Psionics rooting around in their mind."

In other words, I couldn't just try a deep scan of the room to get the information she wanted. I had to be discreet— hence the earlier training.

CHAPTER FOUR

The dining room had been transformed into a ballroom. Everything had been cleaned, making an already difficult room nearly as impossible as the first time I'd entered it last semester. The swirl of minds mixed with the glare from newly applied polish and the scent of pastries and wine. The difference was that the modules I'd built for dealing with difficult sensory situations weren't locked away because I was afraid of what happened when they got loose.

I triggered the BYE-BYE module to clear all extraneous data, then pulled the SORT module to start dividing the important information from the data I could shunt directly to BYE-BYE. Ten seconds from the original overload, I was unfrozen and moving from the entrance toward a relatively clear wall my blue lines had highlighted as a good processing spot. My lines were faster now, too. They handled the important information, absorbed it, and dumped the rest with a tag that would keep my lines from picking them up a second time. Forty-three seconds after I found the processing spot, all the sensory data was neatly packaged in the back of my mind—freeing me to survey the crowd.

The first thing my lines noted was the sheer amount of money in the room. Watches, jewelry—those were the typical signs Ms. King had told us about, but they weren't alone. The man selecting a strawberry pastry from the buffet wore a tuxedo that was statistically similar to one Ms. King had shown us in class worth thirty-thousand dollars. The woman next to him wore a silver dress studded with diamonds. It had to be worth at least three times what the tuxedo had cost—and that was just one couple. Suddenly, I could see why Ms. King didn't feel bad about conning just a little more money out of all of them. These weren't the kinds of people that paid for schools. They paid for countries. Or, apparently, neurodivergent agencies. Suddenly I understood how R&D could afford to experiment with all their little toys.

On a hunch, I directed my blue lines to search for abnormalities—things like how Tabitha always looked down, or how I had to wear leggings under my dress. Instantly, my vision was filled with a thousand unconfirmed dots. They were small things. Non-standard materials in clothes, glasses, and watches, small physical quirks like the man bouncing his knee as he sat at the bar across the room. I stored the information, then cross-referenced it with surface thought patterns. Half the blue dots confirmed some sort of non-standard brain formation. In a word, they were neurodivergent like I was. Every single one of them was better at controlling their quirks, but they couldn't completely eradicate their behaviors. Some were larger, and likely required for proper neural function—like the woman who shifted her weight from leg to leg as she stood, as if she was dancing without music—but some were only given away by the way they responded when the air pressure changed. Neurotypicals didn't notice when the airwaves in a room shifted.

All of them had once had challenges like mine, and yet here they were, not just functioning in society, but funding it! I swallowed hard. Now I had to talk to them—and odds were that they had analysis tools a lot like mine. If I could pick them out like this, how many of them had already spotted me?

Except that wasn't the point, was it? The problem wasn't that I was different—what *was* difference in a crowd like this? Three quarters of the richest people in this room were neurodivergent, so I wasn't in the minority. I just had to blend in with the other neurodivergents.

I started to approach an older gentleman who fit all the criteria for a conversation mark, when a line on my vision lit red. Something in here wasn't right. I aborted my approach and focused on the new data. It was stranger than the massive number of neurodivergents crowded into this room. No, something in here was even more different than that. There was a mind in here that wasn't—human?

My vision blurred, and a program deep in my mind pushed that thought away. Where was the anomaly?

There! I found the thoughts floating around the room that didn't belong here. They were extensive for surface thoughts, and they left a trail to someone. I started to follow it—careful not to bump too many other minds as I did so. This place was full of urbane surface thoughts. If I lost this trail, it would take hours to pick it back up. I sorted the thoughts themselves as I tried to trace them back to their owner. On the outside, in the layer most people would see if they merely brushed up against him, he was searching for an Agency donor. That wasn't at all strange, in this crowd where most everyone was an Agency donor. So why had my blue lines told me there was an anomaly here?

I pushed deeper into his thoughts, then cringed back. Just below the surface, his thoughts were unconstrained madness. He was looking for an asset. The Agency donor would know where the asset was, and then he would use his claws to tear the asset to pieces. She would die screaming.

My eyes landed on the source of the mad thoughts two-point-six milliseconds before crystal walls slammed down around his mind. I jerked my mental fingers away and stared at the man. He was tall and broad, in a tuxedo that bore traces of the same madness I'd seen in his thoughts. One shoulder of his jacket was shifted to the left, one of his cufflinks was copper while the other was bronze, and his bowtie knot was point-two-six inches too far to the right—giving it a distinctly lopsided appearance.

He looked around, suddenly confused as the crystal walls

around his mind finished settling. The thought trail I was following withered like a stem cut off from its root. Then it was gone.

How could someone whose thoughts were so thoroughly disorganized pull up walls that quickly? He hadn't even bothered to pull his surface thoughts inside—the consequence of which was that he'd lost his train of thought. While that phenomenon was simple enough for a Turnip to do several times a day, that was only because they had no idea they even had mental walls. For a telepath or teleprojector to pull their walls up, they typically had to give it some general thought. If he was a Turnip, then how did he have such thick walls? They were crystal hard, and thick enough I didn't have a chance of getting through. Some Turnips had thick walls, so maybe they were natural. He certainly hadn't seemed like a telepath from the thought trail he'd been leaving. Odds were that half the telepaths in the room had felt him searching for his asset.

Someone tapped my shoulder, and I whirled around.

"Tolden?" What was he doing here?

Tolden flashed a grin. "Looks like training just became a mission."

I turned back to see if I could find the man with the badly-tied bowtie, but he was gone. I checked the timestamp on my vision. Eight seconds—not as fast as some of the people I knew, but to have completely vanished in that time? He evidently knew how to hide in a throng of people.

"Crystal, come on. We have a mission," Tolden said.

And I had lost the target.

I turned back to him. "I saw him. Now what are we going to do about it?"

Tolden shook his head. "The target is female. There's a woman here who works for the Company. Smith's trying to find out what she's doing here, now, but she's only an S1, and this operative's in mission mode. She's not giving Smith much to go on." Tolden motioned for me to follow him, so I did. The man with the badly tied bowtie evidently wasn't our target, the way I'd assumed. I still archived the images of that man. He bore a statistical similarity to—

My blue lines went wild, then froze. An instant later, my head was pounding. Where was I? I pulled recent conversation records. Right. There was a woman Tolden needed me to help with.

Wait, a woman?

The conversation records were clear, but the footage I'd been looking at contained a single male focus. What was so important about him? How had Ms. King—because she was surely the one who had found this Company woman—discovered a Company operative, and missed the man who had been leaving his thoughts all over the room?

Tolden pointed to a spot at the bar, on the other side of a group of single men who were using their limited projection abilities to suggest—widely—that they had *fantastic* genetics, fast cars, and big, muscled chests, if any ladies wanted to come check them out. A quick peek at their thoughts revealed that most of their claims were true, but the telepathic manipulation was definitely a turn-off.

I wiped the compulsion away and arched an eyebrow at Tolden. "Are all neurodivergent gatherings like this?"

Tolden looked over my shoulder at the group men. "Well, at least they aren't faking their good looks. Most gatherings have a few noisy teleprojectors. They'd have more, but projectors are pretty rare. Even these boys can't be more than a PS 2—and that's when they pool their power together. Most of the compulsion comes from skill. They must spend quite a bit of time working together, to pull off that kind of amplification."

I shrugged. Noisy teleprojectors were useful, in their own way. It meant the people around them would chalk a certain amount of intrusion up to the projectors they knew were there—which meant this Company agent wouldn't identify me unless I got sloppy.

I spotted Tabitha on the other side of the group talking to a short, curvy blonde with dark lipstick and imitation diamond earrings. Tolden was right about her mind being locked up tight. I focused like Ms. King had been teaching me and moved up from my resting frequency. Ordinarily, I spent my time around the PS6 bands, but projection strength was really more of a description of how many mental frequencies someone had access to than which mental frequency someone spent most of their time on. Before my biocard, I spent most of my time at the PS1 frequencies. I read emotions, sometimes thoughts, when I focused on someone's eyes. Now, I was starting to be able to control my own frequency dial.

I found the operative's frequency and slipped inside her mind—careful to leave myself a tether to my body so I didn't get lost. I sifted through her thoughts, past the mundane conversation Smith was having and down to her mission.

She was a watcher—set here to wait for someone different. Someone like the man I saw earlier? I tried to go deeper, only to stop. The Company agent's internal thoughts were shifting frequencies—a trick used to sort an intruder's thoughts from her own. Any thoughts that didn't shift when she changed her internal frequencies belonged to someone else. Some neurodivergents habitually shifted their thoughts like this just to be sure no one was inside their mind—but this was different. Her mind spun in a rainbow of colors, jumping from red, to violet, to electric green. She knew something was wrong.

I spun a line out to Tolden's mind. ::I don't have much, but she's getting suspicious.::

Understood, Tolden thought. *Go as deep as you can, but*

don't tip your hand. Remember, you're not just a telepath, but a projector, too. Try to calm her fears.

I gave him a mental nod and withdrew—having my attention in more than two spots was still hard when I was this deep into a mind. I turned my attention back to the Company agent's rainbow of shifting frequencies. Slowly, so I didn't disturb the oscillations, I matched the frequency and sent her just a little bit of safety mixed with boredom. The thoughts vibrated into her mind at the right frequency. She accepted the thoughts. The colors around me evened out as she relaxed. I moved in deeper.

She was assigned to watch the man I'd spotted earlier, alright. She needed to find who, at the Agency, he was speaking with. There was a—

Someone slapped my shoulder, jerking my attention away. "Get out of there, 32!" His thoughts screamed the same thing so loud I jumped and put my hands over my ears.

I withdrew as quickly as I could, then stood there blinking at Tolden while I reviewed the footage my eyes had recorded while I was inside the Company operative's mind. What could have possibly made him jerk me out with so little warning? A moment later, a shield—the same one that had snapped around the man earlier—covered her mind. I swallowed hard.

"What was that?"

Tolden frowned. "She's wearing a shielding device. The Company must have found an engineer that could complete the design." Frustration oozed from him on the higher frequencies most normal telepaths couldn't hear.

"I was already inside, though. I could have gotten the information we needed!"

He shook his head. "Unlike natural shields, her device generates a two-way wall. It would have severed your link to your body and trapped you inside her mind until you could figure out how to get out—that's *if* you were powerful enough to break through in the first place."

Staying completely outside my body for long had deadly consequences. I swallowed. Don't be inside a mind when they decided to shield—got it.

I shifted my attention back to the matter at hand. "I got some info from her."

Tolden nodded. "Good. Anything immediate?"

I shook my head.

"Then I'll debrief you downstairs. What about your other assignment?"

"I haven't started that one yet. I got kind of distracted."

"Well, then you'd best get started. I'll be waiting in the briefing room when you're done."

My eyes widened. "I completed the mission. Now you want me to finish a school assignment? That's hardly the most important thing."

"Do you want to tell Ms. King that?"

I pulled up an image of the teacher and swallowed hard. No, I definitely did not want to tell her that the school assignment that I had picked after refusing the last one wasn't important enough for me to complete.

Instead, I shoved down my frustration, turned around, and set my blue lines loose on the crowd. Time to figure out who was making an anonymous donation.

CHAPTER FIVE

Tolden was waiting in the briefing room when I finally got done with the crowd at the fundraiser upstairs. Despite my exhaustion, I could feel the unease radiating from him.

"What's wrong?" I asked as I rubbed my temples.

He turned so I could see the worry lines in his face. "The shield."

I frowned as I recalled the shield that had suddenly separated me from both the man with the badly tied bowtie and the Company agent.

"It's technology we've been trying to develop for years, but somehow we don't have it. Meanwhile, they still don't have access to our biocard technology, but they somehow have mobile shields?" He took a deep breath. "It's not really a worry for today—although I have to wonder what happens when we have to step in and shut the Company down. They haven't overstepped their bounds yet, but it's only a matter of time."

We'd had to bring in individual Company operatives that had gone rogue, and they tolerated that. From what Mr. West had told me, they knew they didn't always recruit the highest quality people—but they were desperate for Psionics. They cut their operatives loose when their operatives stepped out of line. I'd even heard rumors that the Company had kill lists for operatives that became so much of a threat they couldn't be allowed to roam free. But even that showed how different the Company was from the Agency. We subdued and imprisoned problematic Psionics. The Company killed them.

Tolden's question of what happened when the Agency decided the Company couldn't be allowed to operate any more was invalid. The Company itself hadn't done anything wrong—only the individuals that worked with it. The numbers across my vision showed that his situation had only a two-point-four percent probability with known factors.

But Tolden had proved to be a very practical kind of person—so why was he so worried? What was I missing?

"Has the Company been becoming more aggressive?" I asked.

Tolden crossed the room so he was standing in front of me. He must have sensed how tired I was, because he angled away so that, while we could still see each other, there was less chance of stray eye contact. "When I joined up almost ten years ago, we spent all our time going after independents. Occasionally, they were independents who were contracting with the Company, but most of the time they weren't affiliated with anyone. They were just bad people who had figured out a power that made them too dangerous to be left out on the streets. In the last two years, though? Tac 47 has spent over half their time reigning in rogue Company teams. In-Dep has redirected nearly all its assets to keeping an eye on the Company, and we have increased the number of Strike teams so there is exactly one for every single known Company base—just in case we need to take them out. When we find another base, we gain another Strike team soon after."

I factored that information into my calculations and sighed. Tolden was right. Looking at the Agency's response, war with the Company was inevitable. The question wasn't if it would happen, but when.

"Martial Academy is going to be ground zero, when something happens."

Tolden nodded. "And all of the students are going to get caught in the crossfire. That's one of the reasons we've been strengthening our position here. We need to be able to protect you kids."

"Is that why I was given the fundraiser assignment?" Did Ms. King ask me to persuade the donors into giving us more money because we were increasing our arsenal? Did we need the extra funding that badly?

Tolden shrugged. "Ms. King has been rushing your training because you're already a full agent. But even now, you barely know how to use your telepathy. There are a dozen things you need to master before you will ever be a fully trained telepath's equal. Tac 47 got called in because we were the Flex Tac team on call when Smith found the Company operative where she wasn't supposed to be. What *was* she doing there, anyway?"

I pulled up the recording of what I'd seen and felt while I was in the Company operative's mind for a quick review. "I didn't get very much. She was supposed to watch for a guy bleeding thoughts. I got a glimpse of him, but she obviously didn't. I only got partial images from her. The shield came up before I could get anything useful."

Tolden sighed. "Oh well. I'll note it down in the report, anyway. Good try, 32. Maybe we'll get lucky next time."

I shook my head. "Why did you send me in instead of doing it yourself? You're a telepath, right? And you know all those tips and tricks you were talking about."

Tolden gave a whisper of a smile. "Yes, but you need the experience. Canvassing rich people who might notice if you go deep, but probably won't say anything because we've been using this event as a training mission since it started—is very different than working with a Company operative who might start shooting if something goes wrong. It was a controlled situation, so I made a judgement call. Even if you'd gotten trapped inside that shield, Black was waiting just out of sight. He would have been able to sedate her fast enough to disable the device."

So it was a different kind of training mission, but still training. I frowned. "When are we going to get a real assignment?"

Tabitha said that Tac 47 was who the Agency used when something really big happened, and they needed people who they knew wouldn't mess up—but the most dangerous mission we'd had since Houston was just barely, upstairs in Martial Academy. We'd had guard-duty a few times to help transport supposedly dangerous criminals to more permanent holding facilities like the one in D.C., but they had been so sedated that they hadn't even stirred. I'd just sat in the helicopter there and back again, bored out of my mind. The only other call outs we'd had were to support Strike teams who had called for reinforcements. Steele had done some fancy drone flying, Black had tossed some more weaponry down as resupply, Tabitha had set up as a sniper—just in case—and I had done exactly nothing. It was like they were treating me with kid gloves.

Tolden's eyes narrowed. "We go where the director tells us to go. When Ms. Green thinks we're ready to handle something a little bigger, that's what we'll do. You have to realize, though, that a team with a permanent teleprojector is equipped to make some very dangerous situations a lot safer. That means that we will spend more time than you might like doing prisoner transport. If you need to, you can force someone back to sleep. That may not seem like a lot, but it's a great skill when you're in a tin can flying over Lake Michigan next to a serial killer with telekinesis."

I nodded. Adrenaline aside, I was glad we weren't spending every day trying to shoot things. If I had to kill someone, I knew I would never pull the trigger—and that could get some of my teammates killed. That aside, I had thought that now I was a full agent, I would be able to protect more people. Instead, I'd just spent every single weekend training.

Tolden must have guessed at least part of what I was thinking, because he gave me a gentle smile. "Go home, 32. You did well today. I'll see you back here on Monday, yeah?"

I nodded and turned to leave, only to stop. "Um, sir? Where do I put the dress?"

Tolden grinned. "Just leave it with Cal. She needs to fix it up so it doesn't cause any sensory distractions for you in the field. She should have your street clothes, too."

Sure enough, Cal was waiting for me in the hallway, and had everything I needed. A few minutes later, I was leaving through Martial Academy's front gate. I could still feel the crush of minds behind me with the party still in full swing. The fundraiser wouldn't start winding down for another few hours, so it wasn't surprising that I had the courtyard to myself. I took a few slow, deep breaths of evening air, then scanned the courtyard with something like wonder. A semester ago, these walls had terrified me. They were thick enough to withstand a siege, but the place they guarded was confusing. Who guarded combed sand and sakura trees—now just starting to bud—with six foot thick stone?

Now I knew. Martial Academy wasn't just a school, it was a haven for those with different minds. It was a place where others wouldn't stare at us when we had sensory issues that neurotypicals would never understand, and where we could look out for each other. We could find our complements— like Tabitha and I. Tabitha spent her life watching the ground because her visual processing was just as bad as my auditory processing was. Together, I could see trouble before it found us, and she could hear it. Martial Academy was a safe place to learn about the world and begin to practice how to be a functional member of society. Yes, it was daunting and confusing, but it had also changed my life.

I triggered the gate with a sigh and slipped through. It closed softly behind me as I started to walk down the street. I paused as I felt the surface thoughts of two strange minds near me. They were both partially shielded—but not the same way the man from earlier had been. These weren't iron-clad walls, they were like frozen soap bubbles. I could see some of the colors from their thoughts—even figure out what direction they were coming from, but getting inside would be difficult. The shield shifted frequencies like it was possessed by a demon—in fits and starts, with an order even my blue lines couldn't predict. What kind of mind could generate a wall like that? I jerked away suddenly as my thoughts flicked to the dining room full of rich, successful people. What if these minds were a threat? What if they held the same madness the person from earlier had? Should I go back and tell someone about them? I shook the questions away. If I went back to Tolden now, what would I tell him? There were minds covered by frozen soap bubbles loitering around Martial Academy? That was hardly actionable. I needed to get a closer look.

I located the minds. They sauntered toward me, coming from the section of the street with the darkest shadows. I turned so I could see them, but they were hard to distinguish from the darkness because their forms didn't quite fit anything my match program was designed to look for. I widened the search parameters, then gasped as I finally found them.

The first one saw me only moments after I finally differentiated them from the shadows. He snarled and started to rush at me. The second followed only a moment later—and they were fast! I cursed my curiosity. Backup would be nice right about now.

I didn't need to direct my lines to compute the likelihood of attack. It hovered red in my vision at ninety-eight-point-nine percent.

My chance of surviving that attack was three-point-two percent.

That wasn't possible! What could possibly skew the data so far in their favor? My exhaustion evaporated as I strung together the modules I would need to face this threat. As part of the preparation, I pulled the data to reexamine it—the last thing I needed during a fight was my lines going all wonky. Then I shoved it to the back of the queue. It was time to fight. I could analyse the data later, if I survived this encounter.

I clenched my fist to start the plasma pulser I wore on my hand as a matter of habit, and pulled my hands up to protect my head, then turned as another figure stepped out from the gate. "Boys, I know you're in a hurry but you ought to stay civilized."

Ms. King's mind flickered into existence behind me and I released the breath I was holding. The two people that had started rushing at me stopped and looked at her.

Something passed between them and they slumped.

"It is our apologies, girl." The first one said and bent at the waist with a twisting gesture like an awkward bow.

I looked back at Ms. King, whose eyes were as hard and impenetrable as flint. Her jaw was clenched, and she stood with balance distributed for fighting. "Go home, Farina," she said.

I didn't argue. My heart tripped in my chest as I walked the opposite way down the street. When I was out of view, my restraint shattered and I broke into a run.

What were those things? Their minds weren't normal, and they didn't fit with the neurodivergent data I'd collected at the party—but they were different from the man with the badly-tied bowtie, too! What had my blue lines seen that I hadn't to give such a stark picture of my death? The numbers were clear. If whatever they were had decided to finish their attack, then I would have been dead. I'd never felt that helpless in my entire life! How could I defend myself against something like that?

But why? Even my odds against Houston had been roughly 40-60.

I queried my lines, but the only answer was a picture of a creature in handcuffs being escorted by a Strike team through the middle of the rotunda. Her face was globular and blurred beyond recognition, like my father's when I tried to remember it. I examined my memories to see if I could remember a scene like that in the rotunda, but there was nothing.

I rubbed my temples as a headache cracked over my skull all at once.

My analysis modules must be broken. It was the only explanation that made sense. There was some glitch in my brain that had given me bad numbers. It was no wonder, after being driven to the edge for two days straight. Now, with this headache? I was tired, and that had caused a glitch.

For a moment, I wondered which was more disturbing. Imminent death, or a glitch in my mind? My head hurt too badly to follow that line of reasoning, though, so I archived it and refocused my attention on getting home in one piece.

Mom was already asleep when I got home. I looked into her room to find a letter open on her dresser, sopping wet with black along the edges. My lines matched it to a white residue on the kitchen counter, and I sighed. Her medication was open on her computer desk across the room, missing three pills. I rubbed my nose and started directing my lines to reconstruct the scene.

It didn't take long before I had a complete picture.

Mom got a letter in the mail, tried to burn it, then changed her mind and used—of all things—a fire extinguisher to put it out. Overkill, but effective. It did leave behind a huge, sopping mess, though, because our fire extinguisher was a foam one, not a powder one. Mom obviously hadn't been thinking straight.

The ink on the paper wasn't so distorted as to make it unreadable, though. It read:

I frowned at the *Three Musketeers* reference. If Mom's old friend was Athos and the letter was sent by Porthos, then what did that make her? Aramis?

Mom groaned and sat up, eyes wide with her mouth open in a silent scream. I jumped and scanned her mind with the barest of touches.

She was still asleep—but not everything in her mind was quiet.

::Help me, Crystal,:: something projected into my mind.

It was the voice from before—the one I'd heard in Mom's mind.

::Who are you?:: I asked, still only barely brushing Mom's mind. If I went any farther, I might get trapped.

::Quietly, Crystal. We cannot allow her to wake while she is this close to the edge.::

::The edge of what?:: I asked. ::Why are you in Mom's mind?::

There was a snort of derisive laughter. ::You'll figure it out eventually, now hurry. I need your help.::

I folded my arms. None of this made any sense! Mom wasn't Psionic—she wasn't part of this world. Even if she had managed to hide it from me before I received the bio card that unlocked my abilities, she wouldn't have been able to hide it for these last few weeks. She couldn't be a Psionic! So why was there a voice inside her head asking for help? Why was there a voice inside her head to begin with? More than that, how far could I trust it? I tried to run an analysis, but there wasn't any data to compare it with.

::It's a long story, and I don't have time. Your mother has even less time. She's been teetering on the edge of insanity for far too long, but I couldn't stop it. You can.::

My eyes widened. "My mother isn't insane!"

::Quiet, child. I know she isn't insane, but she will be if she wakes up. Just look at her—not as a child looking at her mother, but as a teleprojector.::

I pushed through her walls and into the chaos. Her mind was littered with tools, syringes, cords, and chains. There were faces that blinked in and out of existence with distorted faces and clawed fingers dripping with acid. Every drop that left their nails hissed into green flame that started eating away at what little remained of her mind.

Other fires of different colors danced and flickered in a silent song. A man's face mouthed words in a red flame that tried to contain the green but only widened the destruction.

Above everything was such pain as I'd never felt. The blue lines on my vision separated it out almost immediately and the voice grunted in approval.

::You see? Her mind is burning. It has been burning for a long time, but there isn't anything left to consume now. When the fire burns out, not even I will be able to restore her.::

I swallowed hard as a distorted image with a syringe in his hand stabbed at the air and Mom jerked. The air exploded into green flame with smoke so thick I could barely breathe.

::What are those things?:: I asked through my coughs.

::That's not the point. I need your help fixing the hole that is letting them escape.::

::Escape from what?::

My surroundings morphed and faded until I was floating in a sea of black with a glass case in front of me. Inside were nightmares. Children dying, tortured figures with sick grins, burns, and scalpels, and lumps of flesh. But in every one, there was the image I'd seen before. I started to run an analysis to try and pinpoint exactly where I'd seen it. Immediately, I was presented with the images of the two creatures who had rushed me outside the school only a few minutes ago.

I grit my teeth. Mom was involved with these creatures?

Suddenly, an image solidified behind the glass. It was one of those creatures, more corporeal than anything I'd seen so far. Its neck was snapped, with white bones sticking through its skin. It slammed against the case, sending silk thin cracks spiderwebbing through the glass.

::The Instructor must not get free!:: the voice warned.

It rammed against the glass again.

The blue lines sprang to my vision. Assuming it could output the same force every time, the glass could only handle two more strikes.

The voice was silent for a moment. The Instructor gathered itself again.

::Just fuse the cracks together.:: There was frustration there with a note of helplessness—like she wanted to do it, but couldn't.

::But how?:: I asked again. I still wasn't sure if I could trust this voice, but that no longer mattered. Whether Mom could feel the burning in her mind or not, I had to fix it. I just didn't know how. My lines didn't have any answer as the Instructor slammed against the glass, and the glass shimmered. The Instructor's head, still hanging at an impossible angle, grinned, revealing razor sharp teeth.

The blue lines disintegrated as something moved inside my mind. The voice was inside of me, taking control of abilities I barely even knew I had. I tried to keep still as the world slowed down, and I felt my fingers reach out. No, not my fingers—something else. I touched the glass and pushed it back together.

The Instructor snarled and clawed at the glass, but it was too late. The voice slipped out of my mind.

The scent of smoke faded, and the ambiance lightened until the glass case was indistinguishable from the background.

Her mind was clean. Perfect, like the safe space I created in my mind when I needed a place to rest.

::Thank you,:: the voice said.

I caught flickers of blue and yellow, like a cheerful sky, but they were gone before I could analyze them and I was left looking at the empty shell of my mother's mind.

I returned to my own mind confused and with a screaming headache. Mom was asleep again. Her face showed no sign of the agony she'd just endured and, as far as I could tell, the voice was gone.

::What are you?:: I tried again.

There was an echo at the edge of my consciousness. ::An Instance. Now go, Crystal. Beware the Instructors. Protect the hunted. Never forget—::

Mom sat up and blinked sleep away from her eyes. The voice was gone. "Crystal? What are you doing here?"

I stood there, grasping for some remnant of the voice, but there was nothing. I met Mom's eyes without flinching. This time, there was no tunnel to suck me into her mind. Her eyes were clear. Peaceful, with a childlike innocence.

I frowned. What was that cage I fused back together? Had I actually fixed Mom? What was an Instance? And why had it left when Mom woke up?

"I just saw the mess in the living room and wanted to make sure you were alright," I lied. There was barely a twinge this time.

Whatever was going on inside Mom's mind, she had no idea. I had to lie—that, or explain that I was a Projection Telepath who had just talked with a mysterious voice inside her head that was definitely not her, and who had just taken control of pieces of my mind in order to put out the fires that were burning holes in her mind. Yeah, that wouldn't go over well. It was way too complicated to explain everything at this point—even if I understood what had just happened, which I did not. Best to just leave it.

Mom frowned at the paper on the dresser. "I just received some bad news, is all."

"Who are Porthos and Athos?" I asked.

She sighed and rubbed her temples. "Old friends who want to keep us safe."

"Safe from what?" I asked.

Mom sighed. "The world is a dangerous place, is all. Now it's late and you should go to sleep."

In spite of my exhaustion, I lay awake in bed all night wondering about the voice in Mom's head. It didn't matter what analysis I tried, I couldn't remember any other time I'd heard that voice in Mom's head. When I tried to think about the creatures who were burning her mind, my blue lines only gave me a headache.

I gave up trying to sleep as the alarm went off, and dressed quickly. I braided my hair close to my head with practiced fingers, then stopped and stared at myself in the mirror. Whatever the stylist had done to my eyebrows was permanent. I wanted to hate what they'd done to me, but I couldn't. There was a piece of me that missed the glamor of last night's party.

I shoved those thoughts away, and pulled the hood on my jacket up so shadows fell over my face. It didn't matter how I looked. Better, worse, whatever. I was me, and the only thing that mattered about me was my brain.

Ms. King's lessons were ever present in the back of my mind, though. I could only flaunt the rules of society—that included the rules that governed what looked good—sometimes. Working within those rules was powerful. They could keep me hidden, help me find information, allow me to use attention as misdirection. They could also make me feel pretty.

I hadn't felt pretty in a very long time.

I shoved the hood back off my head, then went to go find Mom. I didn't have time for all this worrying about my looks. They didn't matter.

I asked Mom about the conversation we'd had last night in hopes I could find out something more, but she said she didn't remember it and had never heard of anyone named Athos or Porthos who wasn't a musketeer. I wasn't surprised. Mom's memory had never been great.

What the Instance had said about insanity, though—

I checked Mom's mind for any hint of flame before she left for work, but there was nothing there. Only spotless white.

That done, and Mom gone, I collapsed on the couch and let exhaustion take me. Whatever the Instance had done made me far more tired than I had any right to be, and I slept through the day. My alarm woke me the next morning with a squawk, and I hurried to check on Mom. I shoved a cheese stick in my mouth for breakfast and ran to the subway. I couldn't afford to be late.

CHAPTER SIX

During school the next day, I couldn't stop thinking about the voice inside Mom's head. What exactly was an Instance, and why had I recognized that voice? It had sounded so different than all the other voices I'd ever heard—like a guardian angel.

More confounding than that was how it had known how to calm the fires inside my mom's head—and how it had used me to do it. It was like the Instance had the knowledge, but not the ability to actually fix Mom.

How long had that voice been inside Mom's mind? And why hadn't I heard it before now? Was it because I was only starting to understand how to process telepathy? And, if that Instance was some sort of telepath, then what was it doing inside Mom's head?

I knew where to find some of these answers, but I didn't want to actually ask Ms. King. If I dragged Mom into this mess, it would destroy her.

An analysis report flashed at the corner of my vision as I walked toward lunch—trailing at the back of the pack. Smith and Briggs would save me a seat if I was a minute or two late, and I really didn't want to deal with the crowds right now.

I opened the report and scanned its contents. While I was in class worrying about it, my blue lines had been busy running situation analysis, and this was the result. If I asked Ms. King about the Instance, there was a fifteen percent chance with error that Mom would become involved. If I asked someone else in the class—someone who had been here longer than I had, and so might have some answers—that percentage dropped to seven.

I shrugged to myself as I sat down in the empty spot next to Smith. I was just going to be careful with how I asked my questions, then.

Smith looked at me as I sat down. "You look tired, Farina. They aren't working you to death down there, are they?"

I frowned at the thinly veiled reference to the Agency. Even though Briggs was the only one not already involved in another conversation—and therefore the only one likely to be listening—Ms. King was clear on the consequences of mentioning the Agency's existence.

"Yeah. Detention every weekend is starting to get rough," I said.

I half expected Briggs to suggest that I try to stay out of trouble—it wouldn't be the first time—but he just picked at his food. There were no indications to suggest he was even listening to our conversation.

Well, if I was going to ask, now was the time.

"I actually had a question about that," I said, and hoped she would understand that we were still talking about the Agency. Smith was usually really good at making those conversational leaps. "Have you ever heard about something called an Instance?"

Smith bit the inside of her cheek, like she was thinking. "Not really. They don't tell me much about the advanced stuff unless it's directly applicable to me. Maybe ask Ms. King? Plus," she shot a look at Briggs, who was still absorbed in his own thoughts. "Now probably isn't the best time."

I shrugged and changed the topic—just like we'd been taught in class. "Yeah. What's up with him?"

Smith looked at Briggs like she expected him to hear what I said, realize we were talking about him, and respond. He didn't.

"Hey, Cloud Boy. Want to join us?" she asked.

He looked up with glazed eyes. "Huh? Sorry, what?"

Smith and I shared a look.

"I take it back. Farina looks chipper, compared to you. What's up?" Smith asked.

He looked back down at his plate. "Nothing. I'm fine. Just tired, is all."

I could feel the lie in the surface thoughts that floated around his walls, and contemplated going deeper. Ms. King's lessons said that it was rude to read someone's shielded thoughts unless you needed to, though—especially a Turnip's shielded thoughts. They would have absolutely no idea what I was doing, and that was definitely a violation of privacy. That wasn't something I should do to a friend.

A thrill ran down my spine at that thought. I had friends! This new reality was going to take some getting used to, but it was nice to know that I could rely on some people to support me, no matter what happened. The advice Briggs had given me earlier was only one example of that. Now he wasn't feeling so good, and that made me sad. I focused my blue lines on his body language to see if there was anything I could do to help. That's what friendship was, right? Noticing things were wrong, and then figuring out how to make it better?

Smith gave him an understanding smile—like she couldn't tell that something was really bothering him, and maybe she couldn't. She was barely an S1, and Brigg's surface thoughts were at a higher frequency than most. She might not even be able to pick up his emotional state. But, usually she was better at picking up physical cues than I was.

"You know you can tell us if something is wrong," I said. That little bit of prompting might shift his surface thoughts to where I could tell what was bothering him, without having to go any deeper.

The muscles in his jaw and neck tightened just enough for me to see as he continued to try and stab a grape with his fork. "Nothing's wrong, Farina. I told you, I'm just a little tired."

His surface thoughts evaporated in an instant, and I was left just looking at his wall. I sent my blue lines to try and analyze that shift—what kind of Turnip could completely shield his mind at will? But there wasn't enough data to compare his behavior with.

"Can we talk about something else, now? Being tired is hard enough without everyone pointing it out."

I frowned. Trying to help had only made Briggs feel worse. Being a good friend was hard! I wondered if I should press more—something was obviously bothering him, and I really wanted to help—but decided against it. Ms. King said that it was important for trust that we let others keep their secrets until they wanted to share them. She said that sometimes friendship required believing people, even if we weren't sure they were telling the truth, and hoping that they did the right thing. Of course, her conversation on friendship was actually designed to teach us how to *manipulate* our friends into doing what we wanted them to do, but that just meant I had to be careful to not try and use my friendship with Briggs and Smith to cause any problems.

I looked to Smith to see what she would do to try and help Briggs, but she just shrugged and looked down at her plate again.

"Sure," she said. "What do you think about this semester's Tournament line-up? Are you going to enter?"

I monitored Briggs for the rest of lunch, but he was tightly guarded. He didn't want anyone to know about what was making him act this way. Part of me said that was his right. If he needed help, he would come find it. The rest of me knew just how difficult it could be to sit there and suffer. I'd once been too afraid to ask for help because I knew that anyone who reached out to help me would only end up hurt.

There wasn't any indication that Briggs was having *that* big of a problem, but I resolved to watch him all the same. If he needed help, I would be there.

Briggs was running on the track during Recreation period, so I followed him and started doing laps—just so that I was accessible if he wanted to talk. He was faster than I was, and passed me every once in a while with a wave and a pleasant, though not entirely real, smile. He was trying to be friendly still, even though he was worried.

While I ran, I tried to decide how long it would take me to be as fast as Briggs was on the track. From what he'd said earlier, and what I'd gotten from his surface thoughts, Briggs had been raised in a martial arts family. His older brother, who he'd mentioned in Tournament last semester, had gone to this school, been picked up by Mr. Mccoy and the military faction on campus, and gone straight into the military after school. Briggs had probably been training as a martial artist every day since he was three years old and, while I was getting much faster, it would take me a year with my current regimen to surpass his running speed. I could already sprint faster than he could, but stamina took consistent time and effort to build.

Halfway through the class, Briggs slowed down next to me on the track and mopped his forehead with his shirt—displaying powerful abs in the process. He really had been trained from birth to be a fighting machine.

We jogged together for half a lap before Briggs spoke. "Um, sorry about snapping at you during lunch today." Even though he'd been running for almost twenty minutes, he wasn't even slightly winded.

I wasn't nearly as tireless, though. I could still talk—my extra training ensured that much—but it wasn't easy. "I know you didn't mean anything by it," I managed.

His expression darkened. "That hardly excuses it."

I shrugged, unsure of how to respond to that. He slowed just a bit more, and I adjusted to keep pace with him. We jogged in silence for another half a lap, and then Briggs just stopped. I glanced around to see if any of the Prefects had noticed us stalled on the track, but Berry was busy berating some other poor first year with a tennis racket, and Hunt was over by the side of the lap pool. I expanded my attention just slightly and focused my thoughts in a pattern Ms. King had shown me. This would redirect everyone's thoughts to convince them we were elsewhere. If I'd gotten it correct—and there was no guarantee that was the case—Briggs and I would have some relative privacy for a few minutes.

I returned my attention to Briggs's face, and noted the shadows in his eyes. He was worried about something. I almost pushed through his shields to find out what was bothering him, but I restrained myself. He was a friend. Briggs deserved what little privacy I could give him. I had to trust him.

"Briggs, what's going on?"

He looked up sharply, like he hadn't realized I was still standing next to him. A thrill of decision ran through his body, clenching his fists, squaring his shoulders, and making him stand just a bit taller. "Farina, can you keep a secret?"

I nodded.

"I want to leave."

I nearly choked. "Leave Martial Academy?"

He nodded—that single motion every inch military, with no wasted movement. "I need your help to erase my files from the computers. That way, they can never find me."

"Find you?" I echoed. "Briggs, is someone after you?"

"When I leave, they're going to try to find me. The program I'm in—" His jaw snapped closed, and he took a harsh breath. "I need my files erased, but I can't do it by myself."

I stepped closer to him, taking in the sight of every clenched muscle. He was leaving—that much was clear. I couldn't stop him if I tried. "What happened? Is Mr. Mccoy that overzealous?"

His eyes stared through me, as though he was looking at something very far away. He shook his head. "It's not about any of the classes. I just—I don't want to do this my whole life. My great-grandfather helped found this school. My grandfather graduated and served in Vietnam. My father lost his leg in Afghanistan. My brother comes home in a year from his current tour, but I don't want to go. This is the family legacy—what we trained from birth to do. When I graduate, I'll go into the Marines and serve my time."

The way he said those words made it sound like a prison sentence.

He held up a hand. "Don't get me wrong; I love this country. I want to serve—I would do almost anything to protect the way of life we have here. I just can't—" A bolt of sheer terror lanced through him. He strangled it with the efficiency of practice. "I just need some space," he finished lamely. "I won't get that space unless I can disappear."

He met my eyes as blinding need poured from his mind. Whatever facade of control he'd tried to hold was slipping. For a moment, I was afraid he would break down, but the moment passed.

"I'll help," I said. A warning sounded inside my mind. Breaking into Marital Academy's servers would be a lot more difficult than it sounded. Security would be tight because of the Agency base below the school. Briggs had no idea what he was getting into—or maybe he did, and that was why he was asking for help. Whatever the case, Briggs was in trouble, and I seriously doubted he'd told me everything. He was being haunted by something far worse than a sudden desire to go against his family. One day it would catch up with him, and I would be there to help him when it did.

I grabbed his hand and tugged him along the track. "I'll think about it for a while and figure out a good time to take a look at those servers. Now come on," I tried to make my voice a little lighter. "If we don't get going soon, Berry's going to come over here and then we'll both get detention."

I just hoped he wouldn't wonder how no one had noticed our impromptu break before now. Of course, he didn't have a clock on the top of his vision counting the number of seconds we'd stood on the track and made the other students move around us.

Briggs freed his hand with a tug, and started to jog beside me again. He cracked a smile. "Thanks, Farina. I don't know what I'd do without you."

I couldn't help but smile back as I removed the suggestion from around us and we became fully visible to the school once more.

CHAPTER SEVEN

I sat in Social History that day, trying to work up the nerve to ask Ms. King about the Instance while I toyed with a problem Ms. King had highlighted. The problem was something about how to obtain funds without it being tracked by a hostile organization—like any one of the governmental agencies that might love to take a neurodivergent apart to see what made us tick. My thoughts kept going back to Mom, though, and the voice I'd heard in her head.

Ms. King leveled a quelling stare my way.

::What is it, Farina?::

I flushed. Ms. King must have noticed that I was working on a problem that wasn't class related. ::It's just a word I heard the other day. It bothers me.::

::A word is bothering you?:: The disbelief in her thoughts was clear.

I bit the inside of my lip. ::Yeah. Instance.::

Ms. King's thoughts sharpened abruptly. ::That's a very advanced technique, Farina. Agency Projectors can use it to protect people who have seen things they shouldn't have. Their minds are typically very fragile after that, though. They need to avoid places where they might encounter neurodivergent operations…Where did you say you heard the word?::

I started to answer when my phone buzzed. I looked at it, and was surprised to see an alert from a new secure messaging app Steele had put on my phone. It was from Tolden. "Get down here now. We're deploying."

::Go,:: Ms. King said. I sprinted for the elevator.

When I reached the helipad, the rotors were already up to

speed. I ducked under them and caught Black's hand as we lifted. Stray strands of black hair whipped at my cheeks, and I was suddenly glad I had braided my hair this morning. If it had been loose—or even secured in a ponytail—it would have made the chopper ride nearly impossible. I'd done it before, but it wasn't pleasant. Black pulled me inside, then tossed me a tactical suit. I stripped while Tolden started the mission brief.

"InDep spotted a female neurodivergent believed to work for the Company in a building downtown. Sensors in orbit have tagged her as Nola Copper, the Company's lead Intrastate bomb maker. Only moments after we received positive confirmation, an Agent on the ground reported the location of a possible bomb. He went offline two minutes later. We don't know whether he is dead, incapacitated, or merely had tech issues, but we're assuming the worst."

Tolden nodded to Black, who took up the narration. "The explosive device is thought to be a C32 Intrastate device."

It wasn't a surprise to Tolden or Steele—though they weren't happy about it. Tabitha was blank.

"What's a—" she tried, but then a wave of anxiety crashed in around her and she stopped as her ears began to scream. She tucked her head down and held the headphones with her hands, as if that could block out more of the sound.

I could hear the rest of the question still burning in her mind. "What's a C32 Intrastate device?" I shouted above the mass of sounds. I pulled up a video of Tabitha's reaction the last time we mentioned a helicopter, and nodded to myself. For her, a place like this had to be the equivalent of sending me into a room lined with mirrors, and eight dozen flashing neon lights.

"It's a bomb made of super dense materials that are unstable under normal conditions forced into all three states of matter at the same time. If it goes off, we'll have nuclear fallout throughout the state, and a blast that will level three-quarters of the city." Steele explained. "It's the kind of technology designed by neurodivergent minds that we try to keep out of circulation, but occasionally one slips through."

"Our first priority is to stop the bomb from going off. Farina, Steele, you're the best analysts for a situation like this. Keep the bomb stable until the Intrastate diffusion team gets here. Smith, Black, you're with me to track down and subdue that Company operative. Medina's given us strict orders to capture her alive, if at all possible. The woman's a genuine mind. There's no sense wasting all that precious knowledge."

The watch on Tolden's wrist blinked, and he looked down. "Update: Ms. Green wants the operative alive, too, and she wants it badly enough that she's placing a Strike team on standby to reinforce us. We're to hand the bomb maker over to Ms. King the moment we return to base." He looked up again. "Don't take any stupid chances, people, but stop that bomb. We don't know how long until it goes off, and we don't know if the Company agent has any reinforcements. We're running this one at Alert 3: stun first, ask questions later. That said, Black drew both electromagnetic and plasma weapons from the armory. You have permission to use deadly force if required."

I looked at Black who shook his head. "You ain't cleared for that, kid."

I bit my tongue. Hit someone with an electric pulse, and they would act like they'd stuck a metal fork in the electrical socket—twitch around a lot, need medical attention, and then probably be just fine. The gun at my side was better than being defenseless, sure, but I didn't want to kill anyone if I could avoid it. Electromagnetic weapons could take someone out of a fight for hours without killing them.

I wanted one.

"Not now, kid," Black said, like he could read my mind. I frowned at him. We'd been working our way through everything in the standard-ammo armory. I'd practiced everything from assault rifles to shotguns, to sniper rifles, and I'd spent time designing electromagnetic weaponry. If I could make one, I should be allowed to shoot one.

"Sixty seconds to drop," Steele said. He started shifting things in the cockpit around. "The Remote Link Pilot is engaged, sir. CIS has the chopper. Permission to drop?"

Tolden grinned. "See why we need you in the chopper?"

Steele stuck his tongue out. "I'd rather sit in CIS any day. Thirty seconds,"

I jabbed the BYE-BYE module into place next to the PREP module to force my thoughts back to the present. I yanked the last strap on my Tac suit and jammed my weapon into its holster as we began our descent. The front pocket of my suit held the other required pieces of my plasma pulser. I slid the rings on and let Black hook the wire up to the back of my suit. I looked down at the ground as Steele hit hover distance. My blue lines presented me with the equations I would need to avoid breaking my legs when I jumped, and I swallowed. This was the sort of thing we were supposed to practice *before* we had to do it in the field! Then the timer hit zero. I took another look at the instructions written on my vision, and jumped.

I landed in one piece—partially thanks to the wire that had controlled my fall, and partially thanks to my equations—and released the wire.

Steele handed me a tablet as we ran for the entrance to the building. I scanned over the images he told me to look at and then secured the tablet to my suit. Information started filtering through as we descended the stairs, into a hotel—of all places. What could the Company possibly gain by blowing up a hotel?

I reviewed the blast pattern Tolden had seen in his mind while he was describing the bomb's capabilities, and bit my lip. The blast would level roughly eighty-six percent of the city. Any one of the impacted buildings could be the true target. There was no way for me to tell what they hoped to gain from this.

"Which way?" Steele asked.

I pulled up the plans I'd scanned over. "One moment, they're still processing." one-point-two seconds later I had plotted the least-time path to the bomb in the building's basement.

"Remind me why we landed on the top when the bomb is at the bottom?"

Steele gave me a dry look. "Do you want to be in charge of mopping up the mess when two dozen Turnip civilians see us landing on the street? Trust me, rooftops are better." Then he looked down at the thirty flights of stairs that led to the bottom and sighed. "Except for the stairs part."

It took twelve minutes to find the bomb stashed inside a motorcycle helmet in the water heater room. Steele pulled out a laptop and started typing furiously. "You know I could be doing all this from a comfy chair in CIS, right?"

I ignored his comment. It wasn't a mission with Steele unless he could find a way to point that out.

He rolled his eyes. "Hey, I'm just trying to make sure you know I'm only here for the thrilling terror of trying not to be blown up. Now do what you can to analyze it. I'm accessing the Agency to see if I can find a match. Bomb squad's scrambling, but they're still a ways out."

I shut down the BYE-BYE module and activated its counterpart, the WATCH module. Suddenly, all my lines were in analysis mode. I scanned and sorted the data as it came in. The bomb was a sphere with ninety-eight percent external similarity to a hematite sphere.

I pulled the tablet off my tac suit and held it eleven inches above the sphere. I could feel the pull of the magnet on it, and started to move it away when the magnetic force suddenly spiked, jerking the tablet from my hand and slamming it into the sphere. The motorcycle helmet capsized, and the sphere rolled out—hobbled in part by the tablet. A moment later, it came to rest on top of my screen, like it was mocking me.

Steele's head snapped up from what he was doing. "What was that?"

I didn't have time to answer, though. I pulled the video of it snapping out of my hand and started to draw out the magnetic field right up to the flare. After I was ninety percent sure I had the model correct, I added mass and density from the way it had rolled out of the motorcycle helmet.

"Hey!" Steele said without looking up. "Try to be gentle with the giant ticking death machine?"

Data Incomplete flashed red on my vision. I held a hand out to Steele. "I need another magnet." He looked from me to the phone on his belt. "No way! Go grab your tablet. It's already fried."

I looked dubiously at the bomb that was still sitting on top of my tablet. "What do you want me to do, kick it?"

"You're an analyst, figure it out. This phone is mine."

He pulled his phone off his belt and scanned its contents. I couldn't tell if he did it merely to demonstrate his point, or because someone really had sent something sensitive to his phone.

Finally, I bit my lip.

"Do you want the bomb to go off?" I asked.

"Why do you need it?" Steele said.

I motioned to the sphere. "There's something about the magnetic field that's important. I need to measure it, and the only reliable way to do that is with a magnet—Well, I could probably electrocute the thing, too." I half closed my eyes as those computations started.

Steele waved his hands. "No. Electrocuting a bomb is a bad idea. Much worse than kicking it, understand? No electrocution."

I halted the computations and held my hand out for the phone.

"Fine. But next time they bring cookies down CIS, I'm not sharing."

"They bring cookies down to CIS?"

"Why do you think I want to be there, not here?" Steele asked.

"Focus, people!" Someone's voice crackled over comms. I didn't have enough processing space to assign it a name, though. I re-focused on the data coming through the WATCH module.

I held the phone thirteen inches away from the sphere, but, if anything, the pulse that grabbed it was stronger than the last. The force of the phone slapping the surface of the sphere spiderwebbed cracks down the screen. The lights fizzled out.

Steele groaned. "I knew I shouldn't have given it to you."

I ignored him and went back to my model. Two minutes into computations, Steel tapped my shoulder. As I fought free of the numbers, I could feel his anxiety pressing on me.

"What?" I snapped.

He pointed to the bomb. "It ate your tablet,"

I looked back at the sphere as the phone melted into it, too. Once again, it was a perfect sphere—if slightly larger.

"Noted." That could not be good, but it was more data.

Five minutes later, the model was still nowhere near complete and Steele had given up on his electronics. "There's nothing like this in the archive—I don't care what Black says. It has the general magnetic based sealing of a C32 Intrastate, but that's where the similarity stops. Whatever the Company is up to, it's a lot more advanced than we gave them credit for."

I frowned at the numbers flashing on my vision. "The magnetic field isn't just keeping the material inside in the intrastate phase, it's also a timing device calibrated to the earth's magnetic field."

"And?" Steele asked, "What do we do to stop it?"

How should I know? I placed a hesitant hand on the surface on the sphere, only to jerk my hand back as I felt the prick of a needle on my finger.

"What was that?" he asked.

I looked down at the bead of blood on the tip of my finger and shook my head. "It shouldn't have done that."

A screen unfolded onto the surface with characters all across the front. It was a code. Three of them changed as we watched. Then two. Then one. Then three again. I checked how long it took between each change and gasped. "It's a timer." I shoved the information into the calculations, driving my lines faster and faster. Incomplete or not, my model was the closest thing to actual data we had.

If this bomb went off, it would kill everyone in the city. Millions of innocents dead. Mom would be dead.

Blue lettering overlaid the display thirty-two seconds later and I let my breath out. Ten seconds left.

"The other letters were instructions. "

"What did they say?" Steele asked.

I pulled the images back to the forefront of my brain and tried to decipher them.

"Eight seconds. Seven, six. Farina, if you're going to do anything, do it now!"

I snarled and pushed the half-baked translation into the back of my mind. There wasn't enough time, and I didn't have enough of the code to jury-rig a key. It had reacted to my touch. Taken a blood sample? I grabbed a knife off my belt and sliced the tip of my finger.

Drops of red blood beaded on the surface of the bomb, only to be absorbed. The surface of the sphere flattened, then shrank until it was the size of a dime.

The timer hit zero.

I held my breath and waited for the inevitable blast but, seconds later, nothing had happened.

"No boom?" Steele asked.

I nodded. "Looks like."

He released a long breath. "Why? What did the writing say?"

I shrugged. "I didn't have enough time to figure it out. Whatever it was, blood seems to have fixed it."

I could feel disbelief radiating off of him in waves, but he stayed silent for a long time. Finally, he picked up the now dime-sized bomb.

"It's diffused?"

I shrugged. How should I know? "Maybe you shouldn't touch it, just in case."

He arched an eyebrow. "You think this cute little thing's going to blow? With what ammo? It's my very own bomb-puck! Heavy though…" He paused and looked at me. "Probably because—and I'm just brainstorming here—it ate my phone?"

I frowned. "That thing's the smallest, most dense pressurized container I've ever seen. Frankly, I'd be a lot more worried about it now, than before. What I did—it shouldn't have worked."

"Maybe it should go on a diet. Maybe, and this is just a guess, it should eat fewer phones!"

I stared at him. That was what he was worried about? "I'm never going to hear the end of this, am I? You know, the Agency will replace your phone."

Steele stuck his tongue out at me. "Do you have any idea how much time and effort it took to upgrade that thing to my specs? Any idea?"

But he wasn't really mad. Steele just liked complaining. It was practically written into the fabric of his mind.

I shrugged. "I'm really more concerned about the bomb at the moment."

He considered it a moment, then tapped his tablet. Something in the front pocket of his tactical suit shifted. "Containment pocket. Mini version of what the bomb squads were trying to get over here. Maybe not the safest place in the world, but better than a hotel basement." He grinned. "Now that it's a bomb puck instead of a bomb basketball, it'll fit."

I nodded again, then looked down at my cut finger. It didn't hurt, but the blood welling on the top was dark red, almost big enough to start rolling down the side of my finger.

It had taken a blood sample. Why? Was it interested in blood in general, or just my blood? And what could have possessed the Company to plant a bomb like this? How did they even get their hands on it? A triggering system linked to the earth's magnetic field? Nothing I'd seen in R&D even hinted that we had that kind of technology. But, then, the Company had figured out how to create a mechanical shield. Their technology was obviously more advanced in some areas, but

I couldn't quite reconcile those facts. Just because they could make a shield didn't mean they could make a bomb like this.

"Come on," Steele said, finally. "We've got to get back. Tolden and the others could probably use a hand."

I jerked my thoughts away from the bomb and grabbed a gauze pad from one of the pockets on the tac suit. There was no sense in bleeding all over the building, now was there?

Sure enough, as we were on our way out, Black got on comms. "Where are you two? Things are getting hot up here." There was a crackle and a grunt—I couldn't tell if it was from Black or someone else.

Steele keyed the com. "On our way. The bomb threat is neutralized." *Probably.*

"Good. Because the Company's got an entire team here."

My eyes narrowed. If the Company had set the bomb, then what were they doing in the building when it was set to explode? They should have evacuated all their operatives from the entire city, but this was just the opposite. Did their operatives mean that little to them? Would they sacrifice an entire team to try and ensure that the bomb went off? It didn't make sense.

But Steele took it in stride and asked me to lead the way to where the firefights were still going. Neither of us was much use while Smith, Tolden, and Black mopped up and sedated the remaining operatives. Despite Black's assertion that they needed our help, most of the shooting was done by the time we got there. Good, considering that thoughts and half-filled equations were ping-ponging around my head like a ricochet, and the bomb in Steele's front pocket.

The Agency sent a transport vehicle for the Company operatives, so we handed them the bomb, then rode home in the chopper by ourselves.

"You're quieter than usual," Tolden said.

I looked up at him. Steele was just starting his descent onto the helipad behind Martial Academy. "Just thinking."

He nodded, and his thoughts prompted me to provide more information, so I did. "We're sure the Company set the bomb?"

His eyes narrowed. "That's what AnAd said. Why?"

"It's just that the technology in that bomb was more advanced than I've ever seen. It had writing on it—a code that didn't match anything in the Agency's files." I started rerunning the language analysis behind my eyes. Still not enough information to be conclusive. "I'm not convinced. Is there any other faction that might have planted the bomb?"

Tolden's eyes darkened. "I'll have to pass your analysis further up the chain of command. Honestly, I'm not sure. I thought it was odd when the Company dropped a squad of reinforcements. They were almost as concerned about the bomb as we were."

"What happened to that Company bomb maker our man saw at the beginning of this?" I asked.

He shook his head, and his thoughts were running a mile a minute. Too fast to easily sort out, so I let it pass.

"The Company operative was dead—plasma discharge to the back of the head. Same as our man. We found them in the same room, facing each other," Black said.

I frowned. "If they were facing each other, how did they end up with death wounds to the back of the head? That doesn't make any more sense than the bomb does."

But Black didn't see it that way. He was too busy calculating how high a telekenisis rating the Company agent would have had to have to bend the plasma discharge. "Our forensics people will figure it out."

I hoped so. There were too many variables for my liking. Something was definitely going on here, and part of me wondered how much the Agency actually knew about it.

CHAPTER EIGHT

"Farina, get off the mat!" Ms. Graff barked as I lost my balance and fell trying to avoid Hunt's strike. I rolled back to my feet in a move Black had shown me, and pressed the attack—but Hunt was having none of it. I took an elbow to the gut and stumbled back. A moment later, I was in an armbar. The only way out of it involved breaking my own arm. While it was a possibility in a real fight, I didn't think the Agency would let me use a medical pod to heal an arm I broke in training. I tapped the mat with disgust, and Hunt got off me.

Ms. Graff stepped between us with her arms folded across her chest. "That was a frankly disgusting performance, Farina. What were you thinking, *voluntarily* going down? The moment you're on the ground, you're at a disadvantage. Of all the stupid moves I've seen over the years, that is one of the worst."

I rubbed my temples to try and combat a rising headache. I still hadn't finished processing the backlog of information from the bomb incident earlier today, and I really wasn't up to getting yelled at right now.

Hunt stepped forward. "Her improvisation wasn't bad, though. She's only been here for a semester. Surely—"

Ms. Graff turned on her. "I don't care how long she's been here, a mistake is a mistake, and mistakes kill."

Both Hunt and I were saved from further yelling by the gong that signaled the end of class. I hurried out before she could come up with some excuse to keep dressing me down, and made it to my next class in record time. When Social History finally came around, Ms. King was waiting at the door with a little bit of a smile on her face.

"I heard that things are getting more explosive with Ms. Graff?"

I didn't ask how she knew. She could probably feel Ms. Graff's anger from all the way down the hall. Still, she didn't make a habit of interfering in my relationships with other teachers. Not even other teachers that also happened to be Company recruiters. I couldn't help but wonder what she wanted.

::You really are a cynical child, aren't you?:: she said, then gave me a mental sigh. ::I have an assignment for you—to practice your subtlety.::

I blinked. Not because having an assignment during class was abnormal, but because her behavior was strange. Why meet me at the door to deliver my assignment instead of giving it at the beginning of class the way she usually did?

::Because your assignment isn't just practice with the other students. I had something a little more…productive in mind. Ms. Graff is going to be in a meeting for the next thirty minutes—something to do with her other job, so she won't even be in the building. Now, the Agency has been looking for a little more information on the Company recruiter's activities, so your friends down in R&D have put together a little bug. I want you to plant it in Ms. Graff's office somewhere your analytics tell you she won't notice, but that it can still see the areas of her office where she spends the most time. You can keep one interface device that will let you monitor the bug, and I will keep the other.::

It was a visual bug, then. Exactly the kind of thing I would be good at.

Ms. King grinned and handed me a little black square. It separated into three pieces as I held it in my hand. I handed one piece back to her. She nodded. "Be careful, Farina. Things can go wrong even on the simplest of missions, and Ms. Graff is not a creature you want to cross."

She projected the instructions for how to activate the bug to me, and I reviewed them as I moved back toward Ms. Graff's classroom.

Getting inside wasn't hard—Ms. Graff didn't lock her classroom door the way Mr. West used to. She said it was because she wanted to feel approachable, and maybe that worked for students who weren't also part of the Agency. In my case, though, she was the last person I would voluntarily ask for help. I wasn't about to turn down any advantage that made my job easier, though. I scanned the interior of the room, then slipped inside. Ms. Graff didn't have any classes this period, so the room was empty. I pulled the sliding mirror to the side and scanned the office for anything the teacher might use to deter unwanted visitors. My blue lines lit up a tripwire at the edge of the door—tied to a paintball gun. If I set it off, the paint splash would alert Ms. Graff that someone had been inside, and the stain on my shirt would tell her exactly who it was. I scanned the room again, but the tripwire was the only threat. Either Ms. Graff was overconfident, or she didn't much care about the security of her room. It fit with the rest of the picture, though. A tripwire was easily disarmed. It wouldn't alert the students that their teacher paid entirely too much attention to who was coming in and out of her office.

I stepped over the wire, then did another scan—this time for likely places to put the bug. It was a camera, so it had to have a good view of the desk. Luckily, Ms. Graff liked decor— especially wall decor. Three potential locations lit up, and I moved to each to better inspect it. The first was on the edge of a picture. The frame was black, so the bug should blend in. I placed the bug, then ran an analysis on the picture it created. Seventy-six percent chance of it remaining undiscovered. I moved the bug to where it could just barely peak out of a little gnome figurine on a shelf against the wall opposite her desk, but the positioning required to hide it better than the picture frame location would compromise the bug's field of vision too badly. I considered the third location on the sheath of a black metal dagger, just above the shelf that held the figurine. The colors matched better than the picture. If I hid it slightly to the side, Mrs. Graff had only a six percent chance of seeing it from her desk.

I scanned the location a second time, just to be sure I wasn't missing anything, then stopped as a fact blinked on my vision.

Mrs. Graff was a telekinetic. Why would a telekinetic have a set of metal daggers on her wall where they would be behind where any potential visitor would be sitting? Because she could use them as a weapon if things got messy—which meant she would be paying far more attention to the daggers than my first set of analysis had anticipated. I ran the numbers a third time, and shook my head. The picture frame would have to do. I slipped the bug onto the frame in the least noticeable spot I could find, then activated it. The other piece in my hand activated, too. I placed it on the back of my phone and pressed the button that would allow it to interface the way it needed to. I waved a hand in the bug's field of vision, then nodded as my phone buzzed with an alert from the camera. The bug was functioning properly.

I breathed a sigh of relief as I slid Mrs. Graff's door closed behind me, crossed the room to the Krav Maga classroom door, and froze as I felt Hunt on the other side, waiting for something. I clenched my teeth. While I was sure that Hunt wasn't a telepath—or not a very high frequency telepath, if she was one—she was also used to the feeling of my mind from while we were fighting, I wasn't sure if I could convince her to go away without giving myself away too.

What was she waiting for? Mrs. Graff wasn't scheduled to come back for another twenty minutes, and no one was supposed to be in the hallway. Had I missed something when I went into the office, and triggered some sort of alert?

I didn't dare go far enough into Hunt's mind to see if she was waiting for me or not, but the more I thought about it, the less sense it made. If she thought someone was in her recruiter's office while her recruiter was away, she would have come in to try and find me. No, she wasn't here for me.

So why was she here?

A moment later, I could feel someone else coming down the hall. His mind had folded in on himself since the last time I'd seen him. It was dark, and dense, full of secrets he refused to reveal but it was unmistakably still Briggs. His mind was mostly shielded, although I could sense the nervousness in the thin film over his walls. I caught one flash of overwhelming terror accompanied by the shredded image of a bloodied scalpel—as though he had clawed the image in a futile attempt to keep it inside his mind. After the image escaped, his mind pulled in tighter on itself and dulled to stormy grey.

Hunt tried to reassure him—her mind was also guarded, but she lacked his desperate control. Her words only brought more flashes of pain. Briggs tried to put on a brave face during school, but he was desperate for help. Whatever he had told me about escaping his family's tyrannical grasp was a lie. Someone had found him, and they were changing him.

I couldn't be sure just how much Hunt knew about it, but she wasn't nearly as concerned as Briggs was—which meant he'd likely told her something similar to what he'd told me. I nearly brushed her walls aside to try and discover what she knew, but stopped. I'd been inside Hunt's mind plenty of times before. She knew I was a teleprojector. She lived in this shadowy world the Agency and the Company had created. Reading her thoughts wasn't a violation of her mind in the same way reading a Turnips would be, but I still couldn't bring myself to do it. Briggs had trusted her with information, and taking it from her mind would be the same as taking it from his. I refused to betray his trust that way.

Hunt and Briggs exchanged some words, then left together. I felt their minds quiet with distance, and was tempted to follow—but I restrained that instinct. If Briggs was in over his head, then Hunt would know how to handle it. She'd always struck me as a very competent sort of person. Still. What could make someone like Briggs so scared?

I pulled the video of his passionate face after he watched Houston beat up Smith during the tournament last semester. He was absolutely no match for Houston, but he would have gotten in that ring with him then and there, if someone had given him the chance. He had absolutely no fear. Now, any pretense of bravado was gone.

He thought that they were changing him, but who were *they*?

I didn't have any answers, so I filed away the information and resolved to talk to Steele about excising Briggs from the school records. He'd asked me to help him, and I could at least do that. Afterward, I might be able to convince him to tell me what was going on. That decided, I hurried to my next class.

CHAPTER NINE

Mom was at work when I finally fought free of weekend training. The house was silent. Empty. I retreated to my workbench to tinker, but even that left me feeling unsettled. What was wrong with Briggs? And that bomb in the hotel? And the man with the bowtie that—I stopped my blue lines from running a full analysis on him because of the headache I got every time I tried to do that. It was all connected somehow, but my blue lines couldn't spit out any answers.

I tried to focus on fixing up some of the pieces for the miniature engine still laid out on my workbench, but every time I looked at this new technology I was creating, I thought about the bomb, and then the bug I'd put in Ms. Graff's office, and then Briggs. Thinking about it didn't help, though. There was nothing I could do about the situation and, even if I could, it would require working with the Company. That would endanger my position in the Agency—and I couldn't bring myself to betray them.

I had finally found a place where I belonged. The people there understood what it was like to be different, and to get hung up on the little stuff—like the feeling of changing air waves on my legs while I was wearing a dress. They accepted me with all of my quirks, and were even paying me enough that Mom and I would never have to worry about money again.

The Agency was a safe haven, and I refused to risk that for a situation I was probably overanalyzing anyway. This was way above my pay grade.

The front door opened a few minutes after I'd finally given up and put away my tools. Mom was home. I checked her mind for any sign of the burning, but everything was whole.

She was fine. She grinned at me and asked how my day was—then hung up her keys and put away the groceries she'd remembered to get on her way home from work!

I checked her mind more thoroughly after that. She hadn't remembered to go shopping on her own since before I could remember. And her keys? Maybe those holes in her mind were responsible for a lot more than her nightmares.

"How is school going?" she asked as she put the kettle on for tea.

"I like it," I said.

She smiled—a real, true grin. "What's it like? I've noticed you are doing better. Standing straighter, looking people in the eyes, bringing home friends!"

So I told her everything I could about the classes—even how I'd been moved into a class called Social History that was helping me understand what was going on in other people's heads. When I got to Krav Maga, though, my voice faltered.

"The first teacher we had was Earl West. He was nice. Mysterious sometimes, but he really wanted to help. There was an accident, though. He died."

Mom's eyes teared up, and she nodded. "I'm going to miss him."

My eyes widened. "You knew him?"

I remembered Mr. West telling me that he was an old family friend. I hadn't really believed him—but maybe he was telling the truth?

"I used to," she said, eyes still wet. She pulled the kettle off the stove as it started to whistle. "I heard about the death, of course. I must have forgotten again by the time you came home. You know how I am. What I don't understand is why they didn't cancel school. A thing like that—everyone must have been pretty shaken up."

I looked down as she passed me my tea cup. Mom had been shaken up, too. But she didn't remember that night at all. I'd asked.

I finished my tea in silence and then turned to go back to my room. It was early, but I'd defused a bomb two days ago, so I had an excuse.

"Crystal?" Mom said suddenly.

I turned around at the sound of her voice. "Yeah?"

Her eyes were clouded but I couldn't get into her mind. "Just be careful at that school. Be safe." Then the moment passed and she blinked. "I love you. Never forget that."

"I love you, too."

And then I fled.

The rest of the day passed without incident, and soon I was at school again. Half the week passed without so much as a whisper from Tac 47, or an opportunity to talk to Steele. Even Ms. King seemed oddly absent. Not absent enough to keep her from assigning me detention, though. The mandatory recreation period was my one relief from all the tension. It wasn't entirely a surprise when I caught glimpses of Tabitha Smith's mind following me on the track with the intent to pass on a message.

I dropped back so we could talk.

"What's up?"

"If you think you can make it past Hunt and Berry on guard duty, we're needed downstairs in Tac room 26A. I'll meet you down there." She gave the report and sped past.

I frowned. It wasn't really surprising, but I'd hoped things would stay quiet for longer. Still, if they needed me badly enough to interrupt my school-day, then things were bad. I altered paths toward the pool. The 'No Admittance' sign was hung on the door to the changing rooms, but I tried the handle anyway.

"The door's locked, Farina."

I sighed. The mind behind me was Eugene Berry, the most uptight Prefect in the whole school. Why couldn't Hunt have come over instead?

"Now go back to whatever it was you were doing before I give you detention," he said with a smirk.

I clutched at my stomach. The only toilets in the rec area were in the pool locker rooms which, conveniently, had a separate exit to the hallway. "I think I'm going to—" I contracted in one of the motions Ms. King had taught us, pretending I was about to barf.

"All right, Berry." That was Hunt. Good. "If you don't want to clean up a mess, unlock the door and let the girl have some privacy."

I gave the other girl a mental nod of appreciation. Berry was a hard-line follow-the-rules-or-get-out-of-my-school kind of guy. Hunt was much more practical. In a few moments, the door was unlocked and I ran toward the nearest stall to make retching noises until their minds retreated. Then I locked the stall and slid under the door. I managed to get down to Martial Base without any teachers or prefects spotting me.

The rotunda was busy, with people and thoughts moving in directions I couldn't hope to follow—even if I had time. Instead, I blocked them out the best I could and hurried to the Tac elevator. A few minutes later, I was in Tac room 26A.

Inside, faces were drawn, and Tabitha was on the edge of panic—though a quick foray into her mind showed that she was more worried about the helicopter than the mission. The others were merely worried.

They all looked up as I entered the room. I gave Tabitha a quick reassuring smile—though she couldn't see it because her eyes were closed. If my hearing was as sensitive as hers was, I probably would feel the same way.

Black looked up a fraction after Smith. "Farina, you're late." He tossed me a black tac suit and motioned for me to put it on.

I accepted the criticism and focused on getting all the straps where they were supposed to go, then donned the plasma pulser rings. When I was settled, Tolden stood and walked to the head of the room.

"Chatter time is over," he said, and even Tabitha opened her eyes to look at him. "At roughly 14:00 today we received a distress signal relayed from our long term holding facility in D.C.. Something has happened to breach their sister facility, and we're the closest base with the resources to help." He met my eyes meaningfully. "We're the first responders. A convoy is being dispatched within the next two hours, or as soon as all personnel and equipment are gathered, but they've got to make a stop in St. Louis to get everything set up so they'll be a while. In the meantime, we will first, isolate the cause of the distress signal, second, resolve any threats to personnel security, and third, assist in getting the base operational in the short term. Understood?"

I shook my head. "What holding facility? D. C.? If we have a base in St. Louis, wouldn't that technically be closer?" Those were only a few of my questions, but it was all I could line up before Tolden sighed and held up his hand.

"No. We're the largest base in this half of the U.S., so we're the ones who address issues like this. As for the detainment facility we're being sent to assist, it handles overflow from the long term holding facility. Occasionally, we need to shuffle detained neurodivergents around, and they're the solution. It also works as support, and holds a small intelligence outpost. Luckily, it was nowhere near capacity when it was breached, or we'd be dealing with angry, rogue Psionics. We don't know much more than what I've just told you."

I bit my lip. I didn't like going into this situation with incomplete information, and it was clear that I was missing some background that even Tabitha seemed to have.

"That's all the briefing we have time for," Tolden said. "The chopper is standing by."

Black was the first one through the door, followed shortly by Steele and Smith. Tolden grabbed my arm as I moved to exit.

"Facility jammers will be working to destroy any internal signals. Our communications systems inside will be useless. You're here as our radar. If something moves, you tell us. Otherwise, watch and learn." He held up a finger. "This isn't a job to take lightly. If things get dangerous, you stay out of it unless I tell you otherwise. You might be powerful, but you haven't had the training for this sort of situation yet, and we can't afford to lose you. Keep your shields up, and be careful. The inmates might be less powerful than you are, but some of them are highly trained. If the containment areas have been breached, we could be looking at an ugly situation."

"Yes, sir."

Tolden's slight smile told me that was the correct response, and I followed him out to door, through the passageways, and towards the waiting helicopter.

CCETA's 15 minutes. Want the maps, sir?" Steele's voice crackled over the headphone speaker.

Tolden nodded curtly to Black, who reached between the seats behind him and dropped a mess of papers on the clear space between the two rows of seats.

Tolden handed me one side of the map.

"These are plans of the D.C. holding facility," he explained. "Steele will drop the chopper just outside the missile defense range, and we'll be on foot from there. Steele and Smith, you'll come in these doors here." He pointed to what looked like an alleyway entrance. "Black, you're in the elevator shaft. Farina and I are taking front and center. The fact that we got an automated message means the base is in lockdown. Unless someone else—" meaning a hostile infiltration force, "—took them down, jammers are running fast and hot which means our comms are useless. That's where you come in, Farina. Any reports that come in get relayed directly to me first, and then to the rest of the team. Any directions I have, you will relay. Understood?"

I nodded as my thoughts turned to the upcoming mission. It sounded like they needed more people than they actually had, and I was the only reason Tac 47 had been chosen over the other Tac block 4 teams.

Tabitha frowned. "What about the prisoners?"

Tolden nodded. "Luckily, we're talking about the overflow facility and as far as we know, no containment cells have been breached. Now, we're dealing with a system-wide shut down, so that information could be out of date. We are operating on Alert Three. Be careful, people. I don't want to have to drag any of you out, got it?"

I frowned. This was the second time we'd gone in on Alert Three. I couldn't help but wonder what Alert Two would be.

Black caught my questioning look and explained. "Alert Two means we shoot first, ask questions later. Alert One means we no longer have questions—just blow the place up." He gave a bloodthirsty grin as he mentioned Alert One. I shuddered. Blowing things up sounded like fun, but the aftermath rarely was.

Then everything faded away in front of me as something clawed at the outside of my mind. I tried to shake it off, but it had already started shifting frequencies to match my walls.

It was getting inside!

::Idiot newbie, stop fidgeting and listen!:: A voice echoed in my head. I obeyed tentatively—ready to start squirming again if he made a move I didn't like. ::I'm Agent 97, from the D.C. primary facility.::

I bit my lip, then held up my hand to pause Tolden's briefing. "I'm listening to a projector right now. He says he's Agent 97."

Tolden's eyebrows rose. "What's his rating?" *We don't have many projectors that can contact a moving helicopter.*

I repeated the question.

::Check your files. The info's all there. I've got a landing area scouted. Direct your pilot five degrees east.::

I relayed the answer to Tolden and saw his frown deepen. He pulled a little two inch square out of a pocket in his tac suit and handed it to Black. "Check out 97. Pull his rating, and make sure his assignment matches his story. Steele, alter five degrees east. We'll go along with him for now. 32, ask him if he has a status update on the overflow facility."

::I don't have much more than Martial base has. The only comm activity has been that same distress signal. I haven't gotten close enough to investigate further.::

"He checks out," Black reported as he handed the square back to Tolden. "Assigned under Jane Doe, primary base, Washington D.C.. Projection Strength rating 4. That's all the record we have."

Tolden pursed his lips. "He's Intelligence or Counterintelligence, then. There's really no way for us to check his story."

Tabitha was frowning. "Jane Doe is just code for someone working in intel, right?"

Black gave a snort. "The Does aren't regular agents. They're Joseph Medina's lieutenants. You didn't think their names were actually Doe, did you? But what else are we going to call them? They don't have names—or even numbers. Medina's paranoid."

Medina. The name sounded familiar, so I ran a search for it in my memory. He was the one who had asked so many questions about my family. "Medina is the one over InDep, right?"

Black laughed. "And he has his hand in a dozen other pies, too. He's number three in the Agency, just below Ms. King and Ms. Green."

I made a mental note to re-organize my mental picture of the Agency's structure.

:: I'm sending you my location. You can guide your pilot in from there.::

CHAPTER TEN

Steele, Tabitha and I all waited inside the helicopter while Tolden and Black talked with 92 just outside the range of the rotating chopper blades. After a few moments of debate, Tolden motioned to us. We all congregated around 92.

"I'm going to assume this is 32?" 92 asked, pointing at me.

Tolden nodded. "PS7, but only about a quarter of the way through her training." Then he turned to Smith. "She's been through the full course, but only been on a half dozen missions. We transferred her to Martial for help with the hand-to-hand. She's an E10 and S1 but has impressive analysis skills. Steele and Black are old hands."

92's eyebrows drew together. "An entire facility has gone dark, and this is who Ms. Green sends? What happened to the Tac 47 that only had the most experienced agents in the Agency?"

Tolden tensed, and Black bristled.

"You coming in with us, or are you going to sit and watch?" Black challenged.

92 pursed his lips. "I haven't been able to find anything from out here. What's your breach plan? The facility is in full lock-down."

Tolden gestured for Steele to go get the maps. 92 took the briefing in stride, as if he'd done this every day of his life—and maybe he had. His eyes were inscrutable as he scanned through the plan, offering toneless suggestions here and there based on information he already had about the base. A few minutes later, we were split into our groups, ready to breach.

Tolden entered his code into the pad, and the lights blinked green. He motioned for me to open the door.

3, 2, 1, he counted. I relayed it to the other teams, and they opened their doors at the same exact time. Tolden entered, his energy weapon pointed ahead of him. There was nothing in the man-trap—which was good, because there were no lights except for the blinking red LED on the second pinpad. It flipped to a ready yellow color as the door behind us snicked closed, plunging us into darkness. Tolden entered his code, then rested his finger on the enter button. *When this door opens, I need you to do a facility-wide scan. You'll be free of the damper technology, then.* I gave a curt nod and swung the door open so he could enter first.

When I crossed the threshold, I sent my mind along the corridors. Nothing.

"Sir, there's no one here."

He snorted. "200-and-some-odd personnel don't just disappear. They've got to be around here somewhere. Check again."

I swept the facility again—this time checking the corridors I swept with the blueprints as I went. Still nothing—not even in the cell block, which was supposedly still secure. Except…I checked again against the blueprints. There was one room I couldn't sense. It had to be laced with the same damping technology the man-trap had been.

"If there's anyone here, they're in the room in the center. It's the only place I can't get into."

Tolden's jaw tensed. "No one in confinement?"

I shook my head. "They're either gone or dead. Or, just maybe, in that central room."

"Have everyone meet us there." He set off down the corridor, cradling the energy-rifle as he jogged towards the room in the center of the compound. I sent the instructions to the other teams, then jogged after Tolden.

As I moved through the compound, a chill settled into my bones. Glass shards from shattered windows littered the floor like jagged gems, forgotten in all the horror. They reflected the electric lights as we passed, taunting us with unanswered questions. Smashed electronics, overturned chairs, bullets lodged in the ceiling, and a coffee maker half melted from what could only have been a plasma blast smeared pieces of the story on canvas. It wasn't a painting, so much as scattered bursts of color gleaned from scorch marks on the walls and blood spatter found far too occasionally. I could almost see the person with the fully automatic weapon firing at an unknown enemy. No veteran in her right mind would waste precious bullets on the ceiling.

As Tolden turned the last corner before the room, his weapon came up at a sound in the corridor.

"Wait!" I shouted as the imminent danger pulled me away from reconstructing what had happened. "It's Steele!"

He pulled his finger off the trigger just as Steele's face came into his sights. "Get your head in the game, Farina!" he snarled, lowering his weapon. "You were supposed to tell me when the first group reached the meeting point."

I ran a search for any such instructions, but it came up blank. I didn't have any record of him saying anything—but it was best to not point that out. Ms. King had said in Social History that one should never correct a superior officer.

"Sir, I was trying to reconstruct what happened here," I said.

Steele's eyebrows rose. "How?"

I brushed off the question. It wasn't important. "Whatever happened here, it happened quickly, and violently. I'm sure you saw the blood spatters and fire marks, but they seem to be more erratic than someone in regular combat would have fired. These people were terrified—off their game. They weren't repelling an attack, they were trying to get away from whatever it was that attacked them. There is no question about their success. Sir, I think they're all dead or taken."

Tolden's eyes narrowed. "Taken by who?"

I searched through the half-baked analyses to find any clue to the answer to that question, but came up with nothing. "I don't know. Only whoever they are, they're ruthless and terrifying."

Black came around the corner with 92 in tow. His energy rifle was slung over his shoulder, and his hand rested easily on his handgun. 92 had obviously warned him much better than I had warned Tolden. "We've got signs of a struggle, but no bodies. Some blood spatter, but not enough to explain where all the personnel went. Cell blocks are clean. No inmates, no bodies, and the supply of sedatives is down by half. Whatever happened here wasn't good," he said.

Tolden accepted it with a nod and turned to Steele. "Can you access the cameras? See what happened here?"

Steele shook his head. "Cameras were all wiped. It's like a ghost just came in and took everyone."

Tolden's fist clenched. "It wasn't a ghost. Something real did this, and we're going to figure out how and why before the convoy gets here." He evaluated the ceiling high steel door with a critical eye. "What's it going to take to get this door open?"

Steele ran a practiced eye over it. "This door was designed to withstand a small nuclear explosion, but I think I might know its unlock codes. Unless they've been changed."

92 pushed past him. "The system changed all codes but the outside ones when the distress signal wasn't canceled. The base I'm assigned to got the data dump. Are you ready?"

Black and Tolden readied their weapons, while Smith and I pressed our backs against the wall, out of the line of fire.

::3, 2, 1:: 92 projected into each of our heads. The lock clicked, I hauled the door open, while Black and Tolden charged inside. Steele followed them quickly, and 92 brought up the rear. He stopped in the doorway, staring at the sight. "Well, we can safely say it wasn't a ghost."

There was a stunned silence. I could feel rage pour off of them in varying combinations.

"Whoever did this is going to pay. I'll rip them limb from limb with my own two hands," someone growled.

Steele excused himself. "I'm going to keep watch." When he emerged from the doorway he looked as if someone had poured a pint of coke down his throat, popped in a few mentos, and shaken him five times.

"32," Black's voice was clipped as he called for me. His anger evaporated in an instant, so he was perfectly calm. So calm it was terrifying. My hand crept to the semiautomatic at my hip as I stepped past 92. Even bracing myself for a sight that could make a grown, trained, tactical officer green, the gorge rose in my throat and I froze in the doorway. My eyes flicked over the scene, greedily soaking up details even as I struggled to breathe.

A boy, maybe fifteen, with a missing eye and ripped out throat was pressed against the far corner of the room. He had dyed the once-blonde hair of the woman below him red. Her fingers were splayed on either side, as if she'd been trying to shield him as their attacker had slit her open. Her chest was a gel of ruptured organs and smashed ribs. Her heart was missing a chunk that looked as if it had been chewed off by a beast. Her eyes were frozen open, and salt still stained her cheeks as she stared; pleading, even in death.

Black was kneeling over a man whose stomach had been clawed open and its contents arrayed artfully around him. Each of his intestines was still connected as they spiralled around his dead body. His entire thigh was scraped away to reveal a bone that had been gouged by a wild beast.

"What did this?"

I jumped as Tolden touched my shoulder to get my attention.

"Can you tell?"

His eyes were filled with fury that beat at my already strained mind, and I shied away, my lips forming words over and over again.

"T—too much." I couldn't put any volume behind the words as the sight and smell of spoiled blood battered my mind. I couldn't process this—I didn't want to remember these things!

His lips tightened. "That was an order. Tell me what did this."

I looked back at the scene, throat dry with horror. Every face screamed out in agony. Every corpse pleaded with me for mercy, but there was nothing I could do. I stepped back, away from the scene once. Twice. I pressed my eyes closed against the onslaught of images, but it didn't help. Blood coated the insides of my eyelids. Blood and fear. I turned and tried to run, but someone blocked my way. I opened my eyes to find 92 staring at me with a carefully blank face.

"I'm s-sorry. I can't." I didn't know who I was apologizing to. The weight of all those lives pressed on my stomach like Houston's boot the moment before he'd shot me, and it was all I could do not to gag.

Something grabbed my wrist, and I spun around to find Black's angry eyes boring into me.

"Pull yourself together, Farina."

The words echoed uselessly outside my head as I watched his eyes. They were cold. Every motion, every thought even, was deliberate. He was the perfect soldier.

Tolden said something I couldn't process, and Black's hand came up. It smashed into the side of my face with enough force to send me stumbling, but there was no pain. I looked back to find his lips.

"You're an Agent, Farina. You can't freeze up like this. Now get your head out of Neverland and do your job!"

Everyone was watching me, adding to the weight that threatened to crush me. My knees tried to give way, but I caught myself before I hit the floor. I closed my eyes again and tried to fight past the raw emotion. These people deserved to be avenged. Yes? To do that, I had to be able to tell them who did it. I couldn't just freeze. Black was right about that.

I opened my eyes and tried to pull the blue lines to the surface of my vision, but they didn't emerge. I swallowed the bile down. I reached for the WATCH module, but my mental fingers slipped through it, like I was suddenly a ghost. "I can't do it. They won't come."

"What won't come?" Black asked, but Tolden just stared with disgust written on his face.

"The—" the lines? That wouldn't make any sense to him. "In order to—" No, that explanation would take too long. I turned away, trying to figure out how to tell them.

I saw something arc toward my head out of the corner of my eye and ducked Tolden's fist just in time. He dropped to the ground and swung a leg out to trip me, but I jumped just seconds before his leg made contact. He frowned and pulled his energy pistol.

"Whoa!" Black exclaimed. One meaningful glance from Tolden made him stand down.

That did it. When Black stepped back, and I was totally

alone staring down a weapon, the blue lines came back to calculate trajectory. The weapon wasn't aimed at me. Not really. If he fired, it would hit my right shoulder. It certainly wouldn't be fatal. I pulled a bit of myself together. Pushed the cluttered notifications to the back of my mind for later. The rest could wait.

"Fine." The word was bleached of all emotion.

He jerked his weapon at the bloody mass in front of me and I turned. The lines flicked over the mass of death.

The first thing to stand out was one injury style that was repeated on every victim. It was a slash made by the same dimension of claws. If there had been multiple attackers, they all had claws that looked the same. I set to work rebuilding the shape of the claw as I pulled the next thing in the evaluation queue. There were a number of post-mortem injuries in the center of the room. I took a few quick steps to get a closer look. Claws, again. This time it looked like there were three. They dug in further towards the tip, and I could just make out the muddied shape of a heel. Whatever had attacked these people had claws in their feet. This was the track they'd used to travel from the door to…where? I lit up the track of foot-prints. There was a hairline crack in the far wall. I marked it in red for later evaluation and went back to my work. I pulled the most complete footprint I could and placed it below the claw.

The next thing in the queue was a woman with the top right part of her skull and brain missing. There were scraps of hair and bone dust scattered around her. I noted the pattern. There was a slight amount of the white dust on the victim's right hand. She had been drugged, somehow, before the beast had started attacking her, but she most certainly hadn't been dead. She hadn't died until the brain-damage was too much. The blue lines flicked over the teeth marks in her skull and I began to reconstruct the beast's jaw structure.

A line lit up purple in the middle of a mass of bodies in the center. It was on the bottom of the mound, so I requisitioned gloves from Black and pulled them on as I walked over to the pile.

In a few moments, the other bodies had been moved and I examined the body in the center. This one's back had been severely damaged, but the shatter pattern was strange. I ran my fingers over the victim's back to try to find what I was missing. It was as if an object had been propelled into its back with enough force to shatter—not just the spine, the way I'd first thought—but parts of the hips and ribs as well. There. The simulation formed in my mind. The person was standing in front of me, sideways so I could see the interplay between the victim and the attacker. The basic skeleton of the attacker with claws in its fingers and toes stood directly behind the victim. Its knees were shaped irregularly with kneecaps that protruded slightly. Its hands grasped the victim's neck, and pulled him backwards into the attacker's knee that jerked up. It contacted the victim's spine just above the small of the back, creating the same shatter pattern as on the body. I checked the force reading. 4,819 pounds. Interesting, but impossible with the current model. I started re-working the problem. There was no way anything with standard musculature could unleash that much force at one point like what I'd just seen.

It took me three more tries to get the problem right. At that point, the sketches of the feet and claws were ready. I applied them to the dummy attacker and frowned. I'd seen this musculature model before, at the fundraiser. I'd only had time to build a partial model of the man with the badly tied bowtie, but it matched. Another match pinged for my attention, but I waved it away.

Now that I had the data, I could finish analyzing it later.

The basic form of the attacker established, I looked up. There were no more lights beckoning for attention, so I returned to the other agents, who were circled up, talking in hushed whispers. Tabitha had entered the room, and Steele was back too. Both their faces were still pale, but no longer green. I checked the time. I'd only been working for ten minutes.

"I have a preliminary analysis, sir." I said. My voice wasn't quite steady—I could still see the image of him standing there, blank with a gun pointed at me. I understood why he'd done it. Ms. King had probably given him reports that told him my lines always kicked in when I was in immediate danger. He'd needed me to use that tool, so he'd pulled a gun. That trick would only work once, but it had worked.

Tolden turned around. "I'm listening."

I took a deep breath and launched in. "The attacker wasn't human. It has claws in its hands and feet, a slightly varied bone structure, and almost three times the muscle mass of a normal human. Because of the stronger muscles, I'm assuming the bone structure is also varied, but I don't have enough information to figure out how varied. I would need a sample of some sort. There were more than one. I'm guessing five or six. Maybe even seven. I'll keep working on getting an exact number, but because they are all built nearly identically, I'd need a lot more time to identify and reconstruct prints for each one."

"Six?" Tolden asked, eyes wide. "Six of these things did this? To two hundred fully trained personnel?"

"It could have been seven, but yes. It's some sort of beast. It was eating these people to kill, or after it killed them. Part of one man's heart is missing, and I pulled the jaw structure off of a woman whose brain was gnawed on."

Steele blanched and ran out of the room.

"I can pull more examples for the report, but you get the point."

The part of my brain that was still hiding behind my blue lines, too horrified to show its face, wondered why Tolden let Steele run away, but had pulled a gun on me when I tried to do the same.

Tolden was frowning at me. I could tell that he hadn't wanted to point that gun at me, but he'd done what he had to in order to get the results he needed. "Did you find anything else?"

"There's another room."

Black's hand strayed to the energy pistol he wore on his left hip. "That's the sort of thing you tell us *first*."

92 was nodding. "Probably one of Medina's hidey-holes. He likes his secret rooms."

"It's concealed in the far wall," I said. "There was a lot of traffic between the back room and the rest of the facility by the creatures. If they are still here in the facility, that's where they would be."

Tolden pursed his lips. "Black's right. You should have told us this the second you found out. If there is something down there, they know we're here now. We could be walking into a trap. Still, there are people unaccounted for. They could be over there."

I counted the bodies in the room quickly. "There are forty-seven corpses here. That means we're missing over three-fourths of the people from this facility, and all the prisoners."

Tolden nodded. "That's what we were just talking about."

I pulled up the plans of the building. "I hate to disappoint you, but there's maybe three feet unaccounted for in the blueprints, and that's if the hallway on the other side is shorter than it should be. You can't fit 150 people in a room that small. It's just not possible."

Tabitha nodded. "From the humming coming from that side of the building, the room's probably a secure server room. The computers sound normal—that is, they're running normally. There can't be that many people in there."

Steele nodded. "If any fluid touched the electronics, they wouldn't be running normally."

So not a lot of blood. Right.

Tolden sighed. "Regardless of what's inside the room, we should move. Now."

Black pulled the energy rifle over his shoulder and cradled it as he walked. Tolden copied him, and the whole group made their way over to the false wall.

"Don't harm the computers." Steele whispered. "Just because they wiped the cameras doesn't mean they'd scrapped everything valuable."

Tolden nodded, "Make an effort not to harm the electronics, but not if you get a glimpse of the things that attacked the base. If any of those things are still here, we make an orderly retreat and call for that strike team Ms. Green promised us. Understood?"

Everyone voiced their comprehension and Tolden let Steele past. "I don't see a way to enter the codes."

92 ran a hand along the wall to the left of the door and pressed a button I hadn't seen earlier. Abruptly, a palm scanner emerged from the wall. It was sticky with blood. Steele pulled a pair of gloves from his tac suit and put them on.

"Whatever attacked them used one of the hands of the agents here to gain access. The residue is still on the scanner, though. The blood acts like baby-powder, or cornstarch, and boosts the prints. I should be able to just—"

He pressed his hand squarely on the pad and the lights blinked green. I pulled the door open, and Black was the first one inside.

"The room's empty."

I pushed past the others to enter the room next. Over 150 people couldn't just disappear, and the beasts wouldn't have come and gone from here so often if it was empty. The computers hadn't been touched, so that wasn't why they'd come. I studied the ground. There were traces of blood where it had caught in the beast's claws and been tracked over the wooden floor. The tracks led to the middle of the room and then vanished.

"There!" I found a lever with black specks around the grip. It looked like it was hooked into a computer, but that had to be camouflage. I pulled the lever and watched as a panel on the floor slid back.

Steele whistled silently. "Gotta hand it to you, 32, you're good."

Tolden nodded in agreement. "Can you get a good read down there?"

I felt my way down the stairs and into a large, cavernous room. I swept back and forth along the walls laced with dampener technology. There wasn't anything alive larger than the bacteria, so I couldn't get a visual. I returned to myself and shook my head. "The largest thing alive down there are a couple trillion microorganisms. The stairs let out into a really big room. It probably spans a third of the base under there. That's all I can tell you."

Tolden nodded to Black, who beckoned to Steele and descended the stairs. "Keep scanning. Any bit of information helps." He turned and jogged after the first two team-members. I followed more slowly. The stairs were uneven, and I was starting to develop a headache. The last thing I needed was to fall down the stairs before we figured out what had done this.

At the bottom of the stairs, I blanched.

The room was shaped like a long rectangle, measuring twenty feet on the ends, and sixty feet down the center. Bodies were piled on either side of the hallway, and they were mauled even more severely than the ones in the previous rooms. Towards the center were bodies sitting in chairs. Their wrists were tied to the armrests, and their ankles to the legs of the chair. I pulled the blue lines to my vision—partially to evaluate the scene, but mostly to separate myself from the agony etched into every single face.

"It's just more of the same." Black said. "Let's keep moving. There's another door."

"No. It's not." I said. Even after a cursory analysis, this was markedly different. Each of these victims had some sort of injury from the battle. I crouched over the nearest body to confirm my hypothesis. Sure enough, the skin of its thigh was blackened and peeling away from the bone. This one had received an indirect hit from a plasma weapon, but that wasn't how it died. No. The cause of death was obvious on this one. Two millimeters of hard, silver metal had been inserted into the cornea of the victim's eye and jerked around until he had died from severe brain damage. The pattern of death by torture after an incapacitating wound seemed to be repeated in every single one of the bodies piled against the side.

Tolden and the others were staring at me as I put the body back. "How are these different? They just look like more deaths."

I shook my head. "They were eaten up there, and some of the damage was post-mortem. Cruel, certainly, but impersonally so. They were food that was available, so the creatures took what they wanted and left the rest. In contrast, every single person here was tortured to death. They were looking for something, or they took glee in torturing people and just had time to kill. Frankly, given their skill, it could be both. One thing is for sure. We aren't just dealing with beasts. They have a measure of intelligence—I'm just not sure how much, yet."

Tolden pursed his lips. "Finish your analysis quickly. We need to move on, and I don't feel comfortable leaving you behind when those beasts could still be around."

I nodded and walked over to the first of the bodies tied to the chair. This one was more or less untouched but, upon closer examination, there was a slight discoloration in the major veins and arteries. In the crux of each elbow were three puncture marks—mostly healed, but still present. The victim's eye had a popped blood vessel, but instead of red, the discoloration was black. I closed my eyes to try and wrap my head around the problem. The puncture marks were almost closed, which meant that they were administered before death. The discoloration of the blood could have been caused by any combination of chemicals injected into the bloodstream. Still, there was no puncture in the eye itself, which meant that the blood had circulated, probably multiple times, before death. Also, the way the vessel in the victim's eye had popped suggested a lot of pressure buildup. It couldn't have been in the blood vessel itself caused by the chemicals, or the discolored veins would have popped, or at least swelled, and that hadn't happened. No, that was a separate issue.

It took a few minutes, but I finally managed to work up a more complete picture. The victim had been injected multiple times, left for a few minutes, and then subjected to some sort of pressure inducing device. Maybe Steele could figure out what kind of device.

I explained my analysis to him, then watched as he examined the body. Finally, he shook his head. "I'm at a loss. There's not another mark on this body, so if there was such a device, it wasn't hooked up physically. That's about all I can tell you. Still, it would be much more advanced technology than we've seen from them this far."

I moved on without another word. He didn't believe me about the device, but that wasn't important. R&D would figure it out, or they wouldn't. It wasn't my problem. The important part was that these creatures had access to technology more advanced than the Agency had seen, and that was very bad.

The next two victims had bled out from a series of shallow cuts on their bare chests and arms. It was a quick evaluation. The fourth was different. She lay nearly straight in the center of the hallway, naked, with skin that more closely resembled meat than human flesh. Her arms still weeped blood from where they'd used knives, and her breasts bore teeth marks. Salt stain covered her cheeks, and the agony from her thoughts still whispered to me—like a ghost.

Zach's face appeared in my vision and I froze. Memories clawed at my mind. Hands that trapped my wrists when I tried to get away. His lips on mine again, and again, and again.

"Farina?"

The blue lines snapped up over the memory and I shoved Zach out of my mind. He had no place here anymore.

I moved on. I could finish that evaluation on the chopper ride home.

The sixth and last chair contained another woman. This one wasn't naked, though. The sleeves of her clothes were melted into her skin for the entire length of her forearms, and her upper arms were covered in a series of slashes caused by a very sharp knife. Her face was mauled by two sets of slashes from the beasts' claws. The blouse she wore was slit down the middle, and the skin of her chest had been peeled back and nailed to the extreme sides of her ribcage. Through the bones, I could see her still beating heart. There was an electronic chip attached to the outside of the muscle that flashed every time her heart contracted.

Rods of metal had been drilled through her knees and through the center of her feet that attached her to the floor. Her face drooped defeatedly, and her face was stained with tears. A black coagulation of blood filled her mouth where she'd bit her tongue off.

"Doe!"

I jumped at the sound and whirled around. It was 92. His face was pale. "No agent could have withstood that." His words were barely a whisper.

"You recognize her?" Tolden asked.

92 nodded. "This is Jane Doe, assigned to D.C. Primary. Or, at least she was. She was reassigned two days ago—we didn't know where. Now she's—" He broke off as the full consequences washed over him. He swore under his breath. "This is probably the biggest security breach in ten years. Sir, I'll be outside. I've got to make some calls."

Tolden nodded in understanding, and 92 headed back at a dead run. I could hear him wishing for a working comms unit as he retreated.

"Farina, are you done?" Tolden asked. I nodded. What analysis wasn't already completed could be done on the chopper ride back. "Good. Steele, Black, get that door open."

Tabitha gasped as Black touched the handle. "Sir, there's someone alive in there. I can hear it."

Blood was everywhere, covering even most of the ceiling. But there, in the center of the room, was the prone form of an agent.

His head moved slightly as he heard us moving. "He…help …m-me." His lips moved, but no sound emerged.

Tabitha shook her head. "I-I don't understand."

Black moved to touch him, but I held out a hand. ::Wait,:: Then, to Tolden, ::Sir, this doesn't feel right. Let me do an evaluation first. It'll take sixty seconds, tops and then we can get him out of here.::

Tolden nodded in acquiescence, and I rushed to the agent's side. "What's your agent designation?" I asked as I looked over his wounds.

"3-281." His lips moved, but he still didn't make a sound. Was something wrong with his lungs? His voice box? Or was he just too weak? If something was wrong with his lungs, he wouldn't be able to breathe, though. His breaths were shallow, but present.

His bare chest had an invisible line running through it, like the bullet scars I had from where Houston had shot me. A moment later, I saw the glow at his sternum. More technology like they'd used to keep Doe alive while they tortured her? But why stitch him up and then leave him?

I gripped his wrist to check his pulse. Nothing. I tried to find it again on his neck, but it still wasn't there. His heart wasn't beating.

"How long have you been here, Agent?" I asked, but he just stared blankly into space. The muscles in his face still moved to form words. His eyes still stared at some invisible place in the stars. There was no mind behind his eyes.

"He…help…m-me." I sighed and closed my eyes. He was already dead, whether he seemed to know it or not. We couldn't risk taking him. The beasts had planted some sort of technology in him, probably a trojan horse of some kind. But what kind?

I stripped off my gloves and placed a bare hand on his abdomen. It pulsed slowly, once, twice, and then the interval decreased—very much like the magnetic timer on the bomb earlier. I stood and turned back to the rest of the team. "We need to get out of here. Now."

Black set his jaw. "We aren't leaving without this agent."

"He's already dead, he just doesn't know it yet, and we're all going to be dead if we don't get out of here now!"

Black looked at Tolden.

"Look, we don't have time!" I tried to project urgency, only to be met with more throbbing in my head. Tolden looked thoughtful.

Thoughtful wasn't fast enough. I caught Tabitha's gaze. "Do you hear that?"

If I could feel the timer pulsing in his chest, then it probably made some sort of sound.

Tabitha nodded.

"How much time between pulses?"

Tabitha closed her eyes. ".89 of a second."

"And the acceleration rate?"

"The rate is increasing by .3, each time." She answered. I did the math in my head. That didn't leave much time until it went boom.

A timer appeared on my vision. At zero, the bomb would go off. "Tolden." He didn't look at me. I grit my teeth. "Sir, there is a bomb, like in the hotel. I don't know how big. We have to get beyond the blast doors before it goes off or we could all be dead."

Tolden's head jerked up. "How do you know?"

"It doesn't matter how I know!" I yelled. "We're all going to die for nothing if we don't get out of here!"

That stirred everyone to action. They bolted through the first door, Tolden in the lead, Tabitha following him, Steele next, and Black right in front of me. The timer counted down as they climbed the stairs and dashed through the next door. With three seconds left, Tolden. Tabitha, and Steele passed through the blast-shielded door. Black stopped to look back. I could feel the regret in his surface thoughts.

Two seconds left.

There wasn't time to tell him to move, so I did the only thing I could think of. I barreled through his walls, grabbed the centers in his brain that made his feet move, and forced him around the corner. His muscles still remembered how to run. They carried him the final two feet and pressed him against the wall on the other side. He was safe. I returned to myself as the world exploded.

I saw the wall coming towards me and tried to brace for impact, but it didn't help. My vision went black.

CHAPTER ELEVEN

Someone was shaking my shoulder.

I groaned and tried to sit up. "Is everyone okay?"

That earned a laugh from whoever was talking—I still hadn't opened my eyes to find out. "The reinforced door and walls protected everyone but you. We're fine."

I peeled my eyes open and fought through the blur of color. As soon as I could tell Steele's extended hand from the background, I let him help me up. A moment later, the world stopped spinning, and I evaluated myself.

By some miracle of fate, most of the debris had missed, and I was relatively unharmed. That didn't keep my head from screaming, or every single muscle from protesting when I tried to move—but alive was alive. Everything else could heal later.

I picked my way through debris from the blast—slowly to avoid stepping on splinters of wood or tripping over shorn rebar sticking out of concrete chunks—until I could lay eyes on the rest of my team. Tolden crouched by Tabitha, radiating unshielded concern. Something was wrong with her?

I sorted through my disordered mind until I could find the WATCH module, then jury-rigged some program to make it work while the rest of my blue lines tried to fix what the blast had shaken up.

I winced as the module engaged and my already disordered vision crowded with damage reports. I fought through the noise to find the analysis tools I needed, then shoved the WATCH module out of the way. It landed in a heap of other damaged programs that my blue lines were trying desperately to repair, but I ignored it. This was nothing a good night of sleep wouldn't fix.

With the analysis tools in hand, I focused on Tabitha's huddled form. She had no visible injuries, and it would take an entirely different suit of analysis tools to figure out if she was bleeding internally. I sighed. My mind and the tools my blue lines used for analysis were the product of an entire childhood of programming my own brain for small, individual tasks that could work together to complete the analysis I needed. The benefit of such a large machine was that I could take it apart and rearrange it to do almost anything I needed it to do. The disadvantage was that I couldn't do much if those machines weren't exactly where I expected them to be.

I reached out to Tabitha's mind as carefully as I could, then jerked back as I felt the sheer terror pouring from her.

Tolden looked up at me. His thoughts were a mess, too, but a mess of a different kind. He was arguing with himself about—my abilities? Finally, his jaw tightened. "Farina, you caught the brunt of the blast. Are you alright?"

I nodded. "I'm more worried for Smith, right now. What's wrong?"

"She's an Auditory. The ringing from the blast is agony."

I squinted at him, unsure if I'd heard him correctly. What ringing? I focused for a moment, and then I understood. I'd dismissed that hollow, echoing sound that muffled everything the moment I'd woken up. The machinery that meant I could hear as well as I did had been destroyed—either by the blast, or the impact when I was thrown into the wall. I'd dismissed the ringing in my ears, and muffled hearing was the least of my worries. I was too busy picking up the pieces of the machinery that made my mind work so my eyes would do what they were supposed to. For Tabitha, though? This lack of hearing would be like if I'd woken up blind.

"What can I do?" I tried to yell the words so Tolden would

be able to hear me. If this was impacting Tabitha's ears, it had to be making it harder for him to hear, too. He couldn't read my lips the way I could read his.

"See if you can calm her down. Once she's out of overload, she knows enough to try and fix herself."

I took a deep breath to brace myself from the waves of terror Tabitha was throwing off, and then I slipped inside her walls. ::It's going to be alright, Tabitha. Your hearing will return, I promise.::

Tabitha shook her head. *I can't—* the thought broke off helplessly. *It won't stop! I can't make it stop!* She was trapped inside the echoes of her own mind, crying, and pounding at the walls as sound suffocated her. Every time she screamed, the sound only fed into her overload.

::Focus on something else.:: I suggested. Everyone had to learn to deal with overload in their own way, so there wasn't much else I could do unless—

I pulled what blue lines I had access to, and started calculating odds. If this was being caused by injury to her eardrum, it wouldn't stop anytime soon. But what if I could cushion it somehow?

I reached inside Tabitha's head again and listened through her ears. Then, delicately, calmed the screaming nerves. Tabitha would have to report to the med department when we got back, but she would be able to function until then.

All at once, the storm in her mind calmed. I scanned it again, and smiled. She was going to be just fine.

Tabitha was looking at me with wide eyes when I returned to my own mind. "What did you do?"

I shrugged. "I didn't fix the problem, you'll still have to report to MedDep, and sooner will be better than later."

The other girl seemed to accept that not-quite-an-answer

to her question. "Thank you."

I stood with a sigh and looked around. The essential machinery in my mind was starting to come back together—although I would be busy picking up debris for the next few hours. At least I could think again.

I scanned the room for others who needed help, but it came back negative. Black, Steele, and Tolden had all circled up in the remains of the doorway, but they all looked unharmed. All the immediate threats were resolved. For the first time since I'd regained consciousness, I let myself take a deep breath and pushed the blue lines away. Maybe I could take a second to calm the screaming headache pounding through my head.

Except the moment the blue lines vanished, the world started to spin again. I took a quick step backward to catch myself against the wall before I fell, and narrowly missed a partially melted piece of rebar.

"Farina, you're hurt." Black surged forward to help, but I waved him off.

"I'll be fine." There was a fragment of something—I couldn't tell what—embedded just below my hip. Blood had soaked my tac suit around where the debris had entered, but the suit had sealed itself the way it was supposed to, meaning that the wound was hardly visible.

I bit down a surge of hysterical laughter. Someone really needed to change the way these suits reacted to blood. The color scheme made it entirely too easy for agents to pretend they were fine while they were bleeding out. Or, if they had an abnormal pain response like I did, completely miss the fact that they were injured!

"Don't be stupid." Black said, and pulled something out of a pocket on his tac suit. It was a make-shift bandage. "You'd better report to med dep when we get back, too. But for now, this should do."

I let Black put the white, gauzy pad on my leg. It sucked in tighter with a jerk and sealed itself. I didn't need my lines to tell that this seal was more secure than the one the suit had provided.

"Thanks," I gasped, and fumbled for the painkillers in the top pocket of my tac suit. After I'd taken them, I turned around. "Now what?"

Tolden was looking at me. "How did you know it was a bomb?"

I shrugged. "I didn't, at least not for sure. But he didn't have a pulse. Their technology was the only thing keeping him alive. Then, when I felt the timing device, I made the logical jump."

"What logical jump?" Tolden asked.

"Don't you see? We were supposed to put him on life support. The deadman's switch wouldn't have been triggered until he was in medical care at the primary holding facility. He would have blown up, and our largest holding facility would have been compromised. There would have been casualties, and it would have let the creatures inside that base, too."

"No." It was Black. "There were casualties. The guy we left. We ran away from him. We could have saved him."

I shook my head. "He was already dead, Black. He was being kept alive by machinery. His heart had already stopped, he was becoming unresponsive. He was already dead." But a chill ran down my spine as I said it. It had been logical. Do the greatest good for the greatest number. Trying futilely to save an already dead man was stupid, so why did leaving him feel so wrong? "Getting ourselves out of the line of fire was the best course of action."

Black looked up sharply. "That's another thing. You didn't get yourself out of the way. Instead, you—" he broke off, lips pursed in anger. He looked at Tolden, then back at me. "I could have your biocard for that, if I reported it."

My eyes widened. "I pulled you out of the line of fire!"

Black's eyes flashed. He looked at Tolden again. "You're going to want to take a walk before you hear something you have to report."

Tolden nodded and stepped into the partially blown-up room. "I'm sure I can't hear you from here." His surface thoughts revealed that, although he would love nothing more than to actually take a walk—leaving right now was hardly safe.

Black nodded and continued in hushed tones. "There is one absolute rule for strong projectors. You do not *ever* control anyone else. The only possible violation that would ever be acceptable is if you were controlling an enemy combatant with the alternative being the death of you and your team. This wasn't that case."

I swallowed hard.

"The consequences are very clearly spelled out. If we were going to report it, our job would be to put you under guard and escort you back to Academy base, where R&D would remove your biocard. Your teleprojection abilities would be crippled, and your walls would be shattered. Then, you'd have a fair trial and pending the outcome you'd be shot, or imprisoned—released if, and only if, you'd controlled an enemy under the correct circumstances. This isn't a laughing matter, Farina don't let it happen again."

My throat constricted and I nodded solemnly. This was really something Ms. King should have told me *before* they gave me my permanent biocard. "You aren't going to report it?"

Black nodded. "The way I see it, you put yourself between

me and the explosion. You got hurt because of my dumb mistake, so you shouldn't have to pay anymore than you already have. But, we've got to have the agreement of everyone here. Anybody could report it."

He looked at Steele.

"I didn't see anything. I didn't hear anything."

Black's gaze shifted to Tabitha.

"Who, me? My ears are still ringing," she said, with a grateful glance at me.

Finally, Black looked at Tolden.

"If I heard anything, I would be contractually obligated to mention it in the mission report. Fortunately, I was checking the perimeter, and am only now getting back." Tolden stepped back into the room. "Farina, nobody else could have identified that bomb. If not for you we would all be dead, and so would a lot of other people. Now, can you check the facility one more time? I don't want to miss anything before we head back to the chopper."

I nodded thankfully at his change of subject. "Yes, sir!"

I sent my mind zooming around the facility, making sure I checked my location with the blueprints so I went down every single corridor. Then I felt it. There were two living things heading towards us at an impossible rate. I had only to brush their minds to feel the violence and identify them as the creatures that had killed all two hundred personnel. I clawed my way back to my own mind.

"Two creatures, heading our way. We need to get out of here now!"

Tolden wasted no time getting everyone moving. "Black in front, Steele, take Smith. Farina, you're with me. Keep me updated as to their movements. Do they know where we are?"

I followed Tolden at a run, setting up subroutines so I could keep going as I checked the creatures' position. "They're headed directly toward—"

"Just answer the question, 32," Tolden growled

"Yes. And they're speeding up." I suppressed a surge of annoyance at being interrupted. Still, there was too much to do for me to waste energy on being annoyed. I re-focused on keeping pace with Tolden.

We were getting closer to the facility's exit, but one of the creatures was right behind us. The other one had peeled off—presumably to investigate the explosion—but that didn't exactly even the odds. If seven of these things had destroyed the entire base, one would be more than enough to destroy my team.

I used the reflection off a shattered camera dome on the ceiling to duck an incoming energy blast. ::Tolden, down!::

I pulled the semi-automatic and moved sideways behind a desk with a smashed computer. I looked back up at the camera to try and get a location on the beast, but the angle had changed, and it wasn't reflective enough. ::You got a mirror?:: I asked Tolden. He was just in front of me, behind another desk.

Nope. Not in the standard field kit.

I bit back a snarl. There was a *thing* down there with three times the muscle mass, claws, teeth, and a killer instinct and all he wanted to do was make jokes?

I took a chance and closed my eyes. The aura of violence permeated everything around the creature. There! I dug mental claws into its shields, which, unlike the crystal walls or frozen soap bubble shields I'd seen earlier, were remarkably normal. It tried to change frequencies to shake me off, but I was far more powerful. Rather than tried to slip inside by matching frequencies, I gathered my strength and smashed its walls. Its shields cracked under the force of the first blow, and shattered after the second. I forced my way inside its head and screamed. I poured everything I had into that sound, overwhelming the other creature's mind.

"Out, Tolden!" It was all I could do to stand as my attention was focused completely on the beast writhing in pain only four feet away. I didn't dare open my eyes. If I lost focus, we would become more victims like the ones we'd spent the whole day investigating, and I was not going to die today. Still, I couldn't keep it up forever. I took one feeble step backwards, then another and another.

"…got…you." The words outside my head were confused and garbled, but something grabbed my arm. I tried to jerk away, but it held me fast. This wasn't good. I had no vision, and no attention to spare. I couldn't fight two of these things!

"It's just me!" Tolden tried to reassure me.

"Sir?" My mouth formed the words, but that was it.

"It's me. I'm going to help you out. You just keep doing what you're doing. It's working."

I stopped fighting and let him take my arm.

Finally we were too far away for me to keep a strong connection. "This is…far enough…get to…chopper." We weren't far enough away to escape if I let the beast go. If I could see, the lines on my vision would be calculating my probability of survival, and they wouldn't be good. Still, this was the only way to get the rest of the team out safely. Sacrifice one for the good of the many. I'd already made the choice once today, and it was surprisingly easy to make again.

CHAPTER TWELVE

It was an eternity before I felt the glow of other minds around me. The headache I'd gotten from the explosion had redoubled its efforts, and every second was filled with pounding. The creature had started fighting; adapting. It shouldn't have been possible, but I could feel it making its way toward me step by labored step.

::Brace yourself, 32. Try to hold on as long as you can.:: 92 said. I grit my teeth and dug my fingers deeper into the creature's mind.

Suddenly, something was pulling my body backward. My feet lost contact with the cement, and left me dangling in the air.

The connection I'd forged between my mind and the creature's stretched taut, then cracked. Somehow, they were dragging me away from the base.

Sensations exploded in my vision and in my body as the connection exploded into a billion pieces. Pain smothered fear, and I gasped. My face and hands were ice cold, interrupted only by the searing hot rhythm of blood. The colors in my vision faded to grey every time some invisible monkey hit me on the head with a baseball bat. The whirring of helicopter blades assaulted my ears. Some reasonable voice in my head, unhindered by the pain of living, told me I wasn't safe yet. I was dangling from a cord hooked into the back of my tactical suit, being pulled up toward the belly of the aircraft.

Then I wasn't dangling anymore. Black and Tolden hauled me into the chopper. A hand grabbed the front of my tac suit and pushed me into a chair, then started on my harness straps as Steele jerked the helicopter farther into the sky.

"You've got two life-forms down on the pavement below us," 92 said as Tolden finally got my straps fastened.

"Take us up higher, Steele."

"I'm giving it everything I've got, sir."

I closed my eyes again and sent my mind back down, separating myself completely from my body. My blue lines would have been going wild with warnings if they hadn't disintegrated halfway into my screaming match with those *things* down there, but it was the only way to cross the distance. I forced my way back into their satisfaction filled minds.

Inside their thoughts, I found a name to go with their gloating. They were superior. No, they were Superiors. That's what they called themselves—Superiors.

I knew that name. I'd heard it before—or seen it before. Something like that? I grasped for the memory, but it wouldn't come. Some machinery in my mind—something I didn't remember building—redirected my attention.

I looked through their eyes in time to see one pull a rocket launcher the size of a metal chair and look through the sights. It calculated the trajectory with ever increasing satisfaction. The explosion would hit the helicopter.

I jumped to the Superior operating the rocket launcher and waited until it was just about to pull the trigger. Then I screamed. I dumped every emotion left in my mind. All the pain, fear, and horror I'd felt in my whole life into its brain. It dropped to the ground, and its hands went to its ears. The next Superior shoved mine aside and picked up the launcher, but it was too late. The helicopter was out of range. I let go of the Superior's mind and wandered back through space. I remembered parts of the way there, but the colors were faded and it took everything in me just to move an inch. When I finally reached the point I'd left my body, despair gripped me. The helicopter was gone.

"Crystal Farina, get back here you idiot!" Tolden was shaking me back in the helicopter, and I could feel it, just faintly. I held onto that connection and moved towards it as quickly as I could. It pulsed, fading in and out with the beat of my slowing heart. Then I felt them. I locked onto the feeling of their minds and traced them back to myself.

I jerked up in the seat.

"Thank goodness, Farina! How many times do I have to tell you not to do that!" Tolden sat back in his seat and re-secured his harness.

I could see 92's speculative face. I took a deep breath and shook my head. "One more time than the situation requires it. You should know that by now, sir." My voice was dry and gravelly. I opened and closed my hands, trying to restore feeling, but they were still ice cold.

"We were almost out of range. We would have made it," Black growled.

"You were two seconds from being a falling hunk of metal. They were locked on and ready to shoot us all out of the sky."

Black's expression darkened. "You didn't—" He cut off and looked at 92 in the seat across from him.

I shook my head. The situation hadn't required me to take control of the Superiors. "It turns out that no one likes being screamed at, not even Superiors."

92 latched onto that term. "Where did you hear that name?"

I frowned as another memory beat at me, but I really didn't have the attention for it right now. I brushed the thought away. "That's what they called themselves. I've seen them before."

"Really? When?" he pressed.

Tolden shot him a dirty look. "It'll all be in the report, now give her a break."

I looked at him thankfully. All I wanted to do was go to sleep.

It wasn't very long before darkness closed over my vision.

I managed to get my eyes open as the chopper settled on the helipad back at Martial Base. The straps were heavy and awkward on my chest, but I waved Tolden away when he tried to help.

"I may have needed help getting on this chopper, but I can get off it by myself." I found the release and stood up—careful to keep one hand on the siding of the chopper for balance. I checked the bandage on my leg. Still painful, but whatever Steele had handed me back there was doing its job. It hadn't started to bleed through yet. I could get real medical care in a few minutes. I checked the pile of destroyed mental machinery and was pleased to see that it had shrunk while I was passed out on the ride from D.C.. My mind wasn't whole yet, but it was healing.

I followed Tolden and the rest of the crew through the doors. Inside, 92's mind brushed against mine.

::Agent 32, you're going to need to come with me.::

I looked up at Tolden, then back at 92, who was staring at me with his arms folded.

::Medina doesn't like to be kept waiting, Agent.::

My frown only deepened. What would the Director of In-Dep want with me? He'd already dug into my personal life and cleared me to be hired as a full agent. For a moment, I wondered if he'd somehow found out about what happened earlier with Black, but I dismissed that thought as soon as it surfaced.

::Look, 92, I just got blown up. What's so important that it can't wait until I get this piece of building out of my leg?::

92 didn't bother to hide his annoyance. ::You aren't going to find out unless you come.::

I shelved thoughts of MedDep and followed 92 down to the rotunda and back up the InDep elevator—my leg throbbing the whole way. Why couldn't they just connect the four sections of the building and have done with it? My map of the base showed that the chopper pad was only a four minute walk to the InDep section, except there was a wall in the way. With the wall, it took almost fifteen minutes to take the elevator up to the rotunda, then back down into InDep.

I shoved away the calculations that showed the increase in defensibility with a grunt. Defensible or not, I just wanted to be done with this.

92 finally slowed in front of an unlabeled InDep door with an armed Tac officer in front. He looked at us with critical indifference as we approached.

"Agents 92 and 32 for Medina," 92 said, coming to a stop. I leaned against the wall a moment to take the pressure off my throbbing leg. Those painkillers were starting to wear off. I considered taking another one, but decided against it. Who knew what MedDep was going to want to pump me full of when I finally made it across the compound again.

The Tac officer pulled a three by two inch electronic device off his suit and looked at it a moment. Then he blinked. "92, you're assigned to the Primary D.C. holding area. What are you doing here?"

92 pursed his lips, but his mind was closed so I couldn't tell whether it was from annoyance or pain. "My superior officer was KIA. Director Medina has requested an in-person report."

The Tac officer had just looked down at his screen to verify when Medina strode down the hall in his typical white collared shirt.

"Agent 92, I'm glad you're back in one piece. You have the intel I requested?" His eyes were focused on 92 with an intensity that made me shudder, and I found myself looking down at the floor to avoid his gaze. He seemed different today, now that I knew he was the third ranking individual in the Agency. Even from outside his shields, I could feel his mind. He was so powerful that he couldn't help spilling out to take in everything around him. If I found his eyes, I could get trapped in that mind the same way I got trapped in Mom's.

"Sir?" The Tac agent raised an eyebrow.

"Let them in, Anderson," Medina said.

Anderson stepped aside and tensed to a sort of attention. It was less formal than Castillo's military stance, but every bit as present. I wondered where he'd learned that mannerism. The Agency tended to try and stay as separate from governmental militaries as they could. One of the reasons the Agency regulated neurodivergents was to keep Turnips, and governments, from finding out about us. As such, the Agency could hardly recruit from militaries. If they did, it would have to be far more subtle than the recruitment process at Martial Academy. Of course, it was possible that Ms. King's program here was far more subtle than I gave it credit for. Not all the individuals at Martial Academy had my arsenal of analysis skills.

I archived that train of thought for later as Medina led the way into his office.

The room wasn't large—perhaps half the size of Ms. King's office upstairs—with only a single cabinet on the right wall that held a variety of weapons. Most of those were things that had been on the neurotypical market at one point in time. I recognized a Walther PPK mounted next to a larger caliber weapon I'd never seen before. The wall behind the desk felt subtly wrong so I pulled the blue lines to the forefront of my vision. They matched it with my mostly complete map of the facility and reported a ninety-six percent chance that it was a false wall. It was missing three feet of space, oddly reminiscent of the false wall back in D.C..

I shuddered and banished the blue lines as my headache from earlier threatened to crash over my brain—which was only my just desserts. The mess inside my mind wasn't quite cleaned up, and every time I pulled on my blue lines, I had to create bypasses to bridge across modules that were still missing pieces, which only further lengthened the time until I was back in one piece.

92 seated himself in one of the two chairs across the desk, and motioned for me to do the same. I just stared at him as I battled growing dislike. He had made me walk here with a chunk of building stuck in my leg, and now he was telling me to sit down, like a good little girl. Well, I was fed up with it. I clenched my jaw and folded my arms over my chest—waiting for an explanation.

Medina closed the door, then found his way to the other side of the desk. His eyes studied mine, although I tried my best to avoid him by looking down at the desk. I wondered if he saw the building anger in my mind, or if the walls I was working so hard on learning to hold actually kept him out. Finally, he looked at 92. "She isn't one of my agents. What's she doing here?"

What a great question! I glared at 92. Evidently I hadn't been keeping anyone waiting. 92 must have made it up just to get me here. I opened my mouth to ask him a scathing question, but a twitch of Medina's finger silenced me.

92's expression went bland. "This is Crystal Farina, Agent 32. She's a Projector Telepath with PS 7, currently located at TacDep."

Medina nodded. "I know that, but it doesn't explain what she's doing in this briefing."

92 held up a hand. "She's also a visual eidetic with an im-

pressive amount of analysis skill. She's here to supplement the report."

"Ah." That seemed to mollify him. "So what about my Doe? Over the comms, you promised me a full report."

92 looked down at his hands, clasped in his lap. "Tac 47 and I entered the base around 16:25." He looked at me to verify the time, then waited while I sorted through the video files.

"16:32." I made the words as terse as I could. Some of my audio tools were still mixed in with the rest of the broken machinery, so I couldn't tell how successful I was.

Medina arched an eyebrow, but didn't say anything.

"The entire base appeared to be deserted until Agent 32 picked up an area she couldn't sense. We met at the doors. I used override codes to open the door. This is what we found." 92 produced a tablet and laid it on the desk. "Sir, requesting use of your interface device."

Medina rocked back in his chair and thought for a moment. Then he frowned. "Granted."

A device that looked like a hand-scanner floated off the bookshelf and onto the desk. 92 connected it to the tablet with a thin, spiderweb-like wire.

"Agent 32, if you would place your hand here please?"

"Why should I?" I addressed the question to 92, whose eyes hardened.

"Because the Director of InDep asked you to," he said mildly. I couldn't tell which was worse—the fact that he'd dodged the question, or that he'd used Medina to do it. Again.

Medina pushed the device closer to me. "This interface device will allow us to see through your mind's eye. Working with someone who is not a visual edetic, it would let us see what they saw during the mission. In this case, it will let us see everything, down to models you constructed in your mind."

Which was the easiest way for me to pass on the analysis I'd done during the mission, I conceded.

That didn't mean I had to like 92's attitude about it.

I put my hand inside the imprint on the side of the device. "What next?"

Medina gave a gentle smile. "Just go back in your memory to your analysis of the first room."

I didn't bother to hide my groan. This was going to leave me with a headache of massive proportions.

Medina's eyes narrowed. "What's wrong?"

I glared at 92 again. "I got blown up, sir. These analysis tools you want to see? I have to dig each one out of a trash heap of broken machines, then fix and reinstall it before I can do anything."

Wordlessly, Medina pulled a little white pill from the top drawer of his desk and offered it to me.

"What is it?"

92 snorted. "A fast acting stimulant. It's what we give our analysts when they're on a time crunch. Perfectly safe—even for newbies."

I grit my teeth and took the pill. A moment later, my blue lines perked up. Soon, my mind was more-or-less back in order. The stimulant might have helped me fix myself, but it wasn't as good at smothering my headache as I had hoped. My head throbbed in time with my heartbeat as I finally found my way back to the start of the mission.

I sifted through the video feed as quickly as I could and started playing at the beginning of my analysis. I skipped the part where Tolden pulled a gun.

The tablet displayed a projection of the memory, which Medina watched with interest. When I pulled the simulation of a Superior physical structure, he held his hand up.

"Stop there." He frowned at me and sought my eyes again, but I looked down at his desk. The last thing I needed was to be caught up in his mind. My forehead already felt like it was being slowly crushed in by gravity, and I wasn't sure I could keep a hold of myself this time. "Did you ever actually see one of these with your own eyes?"

I nodded—slowly so I didn't further agitate my head.

The intensity of his mind only grew.

"Three times. Once during the fundraiser, once outside the Academy on my way home from school, and again while I was in another one's head."

I pulled the second instance of the Superior priming its launcher to shoot the helicopter down.

I felt portions of Medina's surface thoughts turning to another, similar creature we had in the Agency right now. Then his walls snapped up hard enough to give me whiplash. In an instant, the sense of his mind vanished, leaving me blind. It took a moment to blink away the shock. When I'd recovered, Medina motioned for me to move on. While he must have known what had just happened, he didn't look at all sorry for the way he'd just doubled my headache.

I sped through most of the next piece, until I found the image of Jane Doe. I showed them what analysis I'd completed while I fought off my churning stomach—although I couldn't tell how much of the nausea was from the memory and how much was from the pain building in both my head and leg. "If you'd like, I can run a deeper analysis." Later. Much later. When my head didn't feel like it was going to fall off.

But he was already shaking his head. "That's enough. My analysts can take it from there. I want to know what you think of the whole thing, though."

I clenched my fists. The only thing I thought of that encounter was that I was glad it was finished, and I was free to get to MedDep—oh wait. I couldn't get proper medical care until Director Medina let me go. "What I think is all there in the analysis, sir." It was a struggle to keep my tone civil.

His eyes narrowed. "Don't tell me you don't have any theories about what happened."

I risked a quick look up, to find his face as unreadable as ever. If I wanted out of here, I was going to have to give him something. I took a deep breath, hoping that the extra oxygen would calm my screaming head. It didn't.

"Well, she was tortured. I can say that with ninety-nine-point-nine percent accuracy. I didn't have much time to evaluate it, and all the evidence is gone now, but I'd like to draw your attention to the device attached to her heart." I pulled the image and let it play as a recording for several seconds. Then I snatched my hand back. "Her heart was still beating. My guess is that she died from blood loss. The cuts on her arm, and her face, and the way her skin and muscle was pulled out like that make bleeding out inevitable. Otherwise, she likely would have still been alive when we arrived. Similar technology was used in the bomber."

92 and Medina exchanged a meaningful glance, but both their minds were shut up so tight I couldn't tell what they were saying.

Finally, Medina sighed. "Thank you, Agent. Now report to MedDep and see to that leg."

I winced as I put pressure on my leg. The painkillers were definitely out of my system, and the stimulant was *not* helping. I could see why they didn't hand those out to analysts in the field. I went back down the hall at my best pace without thanking them.

Despite the knowledge that keeping my analysis of the

previous conversation to a minimum was my best chance at calming my headache, I couldn't help myself. Medina and 92 had known something about the Superiors—more than they were letting on. Was the Agency connected to them somehow? Why had the Superiors tortured Jane Doe? Could it have something to do with the asset the Superior at the fundraiser was looking for? What about the missing prisoners? They hadn't even asked about them.

I choked down the bile as an image of that blood washed room invaded my vision. Suddenly my analysis of the Superiors outside the Academy made more sense. Without Ms. King's intervention, I wouldn't have made it home alive. But why? And if they were so dangerous, then why wasn't the Agency regulating them? What even were they?

I swiped my card and stepped into the elevator. Robbins, the teleprojector who had vetted my memories during my first time at the Agency, was waiting inside.

I pressed the button that would take me back to the rotunda and ignored him. Maybe he would go away.

The social niceties program pinged at me, and I contemplated tearing it out of the framework and hurling it against the wall of my mind—except that would hurt. Why, of all the programs to be already repaired, had my blue lines made the social niceties program a priority?

It pinged a second time, and I growled at it.

"Is everything alright, 32?" Robbins asked mildly. "You seem distressed."

I ran a hand through my hair. "Not distressed," I lied. "Just tired." And not feeling up to having a conversation right now. There were too many puzzle pieces I needed to connect, and too many pieces of my mind that *hurt*.

Robbins nodded. "I'm glad I ran into you," he said as the elevator door opened and I tried to limp away. He followed me. "I wanted to see how you were settling into the Agency. You seemed overwhelmed the last time I saw you. Are things making a little more sense, now?"

More sense? Every time I turned around, there was another puzzle piece that didn't quite fit. Human-esque monsters calling themselves Superiors? What was next, aliens? It didn't help that Medina was being cagey, and my brain resembled the wreckage of the base we'd left behind.

I bit down all the words I wanted to say and took a deep breath. "Yeah, I'm settling in fine." That was certainly what he wanted to hear. Maybe he would leave me alone long enough for me to find my way to MedDep before I passed out in the middle of the rotunda.

Robbins caught my arm as I swayed on my feet. "Here, let me help you to MedDep, and you can tell me about what you think of your new team."

A moment later, I was standing in front of the counter at MedDep, blinking at the waiting room. I looked around for Robbins, but he was gone. I shook my head. I must have spaced out for a while. I limped forward a few steps to catch the attention of the white-uniformed man at the front counter.

"Can I help you?" he asked.

I nodded. "I think I have a piece of building in my leg." I suppressed a bubble of irrational laughter. It wasn't really funny—but it did *hurt*.

The man's eyes widened as he punched a few numbers into the computer. "Crazy tac lad..." he murmured as he came around the counter to take a look.

CHAPTER THIRTEEN

The next few days were filled with headaches and incomplete data as I tried to sift through the analysis I had stacked up in my queue. Part of it was due to the damaged machinery in my mind—which was mostly healed, but still disordered enough to cause occasional snags. I could trace the rest of the incomplete data partway through my mind, and then the trail stopped. Inevitably, chasing after the holes in my mind left me with a headache, so I stopped looking after a while.

To distract myself from my still healing mind, I thought about Briggs and the servers he wanted me to break into. I'd snooped around some after my last mission with Tac 47, and found that the security measures weren't quite as heavy as I'd anticipated. Between the codes found on the Agency card that let me move freely in the base below, and Steele's hacking skills, it wouldn't take much to remove Briggs's records from the system. Now the only thing I needed to do was convince Steele to help.

I checked the time at the top of my vision and winced. Ms. Graff was getting better at timing her errands. The seven minutes I'd been counting on to be able to go down and ask Steele about helping break into the server had dwindled to two—which was enough time to get to the rotunda if I ran, but hardly enough to ask Steele to help, then get back to Martial Academy in time for my next class.

Perhaps I could just miss the first part of Mr. O'Brien's Psychology class today. He would give me detention, but I would probably get detention from Ms. King anyway. Of course, there was a huge difference between getting detention from a happy Ms. King and an unhappy Ms. King—and she wouldn't like it if I started skipping classes for anything other than Agency business.

I turned around to start back toward Mr. O'Brien's class as the gong rang. My phone gave three short buzzes against my leg, and I stifled a sigh. Those buzzes indicated an Agency-related alert. I pulled it out of my pocket, expecting some sort of notification from Steele's messaging app. Instead, it was a message from the little black bug I'd stuck on the back of the phone. There had been movement in Ms. Graff's office. I tapped the notification and watched as the external door to Ms. Graff's office opened to admit Ms. Green.

Well, that was odd.

Ms. Green was the director of both Martial Academy and the Agency. As such, she was the single most powerful person in the building. So what was she doing in Ms. Graff's office?

The bug notified me every once in a while, but Ms. Graff did a very good job of separating Martial Academy business from Company business. She hadn't been up to anything useful so far, so I usually ignored the feed. The blue lines on my vision flashed a ninety-eight-point-two percent chance that Ms. Green wasn't there to talk about Martial Academy business as the gong rang to signal the end of the martial period. Another quick computation showed that Ms. King wouldn't have a problem if I missed the first part of my next class. Agency matters took precedence over the schoolwork I could always make up this weekend.

I hurried back to the dormitories so no one would catch me skipping class while I watched the phone. Ms. Graff entered her office just moments after I made it to my bed.

Ms. Green turned so I could see her lips. "What is so important that we couldn't meet in my office?"

Ms. Graff said something I couldn't see. Ms. Green's lips thinned. "Ambushing me in my own school is hardly wise."

Ms. Graff moved to the other side of the desk, and motioned for Ms. Green to sit down. She did so—and then her back was to the camera.

"Besides, if you really thought this was an ambush, you wouldn't have come alone—so let's dispense with the allegations. You're here because you want to know what we've been doing, and he's here because we want to be taken seriously."

Ms. Green looked over her shoulder, toward a corner of the room where the camera didn't reach. She paled. "I see. Well, I'm listening."

Ms. Graff smiled. "You've been picking up some of our operatives—ones who haven't done a thing to you or anyone else. That needs to stop now."

Ms. Green turned back to face the desk, so I couldn't see her reply, but Ms. Graff nodded.

"That is understandably unfortunate, and something we intend to remedy. You see, we aren't chasing you. Your agents and donors just happen to be in the way of our actual targets. There is an organization that exists in the shadows. You're only starting to get a taste of what they can do, but they have destroyed dozens of our bases, and killed thousands of our operatives. We have no illusions."

Ms. Green stood, and turned to address the person standing in the corner. "You really expect me to believe that the devastation you're leaving behind is justified? I don't care what the Company's mission is, or who you're fighting. You leave an unacceptable amount of destruction in your wake. If you tone down your operations, then we'll downgrade your threat levels. Otherwise, we'll continue to bring in any operative that is deemed a threat."

"You can't possibly be that naive," Ms. Graff spat. Then she stopped—likely due to a cue from the person standing in the corner.

Ms. Green was shaking her head. "Threat or not, it's none of our business. If the Turnips find out about Psionics because of your reckless operations, there will be no going back. I am not going to be responsible for the mass chaos that will ensue if that happens. If that means I have to lock up every single one of you—yes, even you, Director—then I will. You will stay out of our way, and tone down your operations. I won't ask so nicely again."

She started to leave, only to stop as Ms. Graff pounded her fist on her desk.

"They're taking Turnips now, not just neurodivergents. Are you blind? This is the Institute we're talking about! They don't want to keep this secret—well at least we're trying. Having to work around you doesn't mean we do it more quietly, it just means more Turnips get hurt, and the Institute gets more fodder for their experiments. If we don't nip this in the bud, it's going to get a whole lot worse."

"And if you escalate to open warfare, even more Turnips will get caught in the middle. Now I have a dozen other meetings. Elaine, I will see you at the next staff meeting and, Director," she inclined her head, although her eyes were spitting fire, "Stay out of our way."

She strode out of the room, leaving a shocked Ms. Graff behind.

A man stepped out of the corner, but the angle was too steep for me to see his face.

Ms. Graff nodded. "Yeah, that could have gone better. What are we going to do now?"

He turned to leave the room, and I gasped. The picture of his face through the camera was so blurred, I couldn't make out a single detail.

Ms. Graff stiffened to attention. "Yes, Director."

He left.

I bolted from the dorm room, headed for the hallways the man would have to take in order to get back outside. While I ran, my thoughts raced. His blurry face had to be caused by some sort of electronic interference, right? Making a device that would blur camera recordings was stupidly simple. For a moment, I wondered why he would care about being caught on camera, but then I shrugged. As the director of such a powerful organization, he probably needed to be very careful about where he was seen. A clandestine meeting with the Agency's Director probably wasn't something he wanted recorded.

There was a part of me that desperately needed to see his face. I wanted to see the person who had put together the organization that recruited so indiscriminately, and who had employed Earl West.

I calculated his last known speed and set up a path that would put me on an intercept with him—but when I reached the spot where our paths should have crossed, he was gone. I spent the next ten minutes searching the hallways, but to no avail. I looked back at the screen on my phone that showed a now-empty office. The Company's Director was a ghost.

I re-checked my calculations, but it didn't help. The director should have been right here!

A timer in the corner of my vision flashed, reminding me that I was currently missing class. I looked back at the phone one more time, then archived the footage. That would come in handy later, face or no face. I stowed the phone and strode toward Mr. O'Brien's class.

During the rest of the day's classes, I analyzed the video of Ms. Green's meeting with Ms. Graff and the Company's Director, but it yielded little extra information. Who was the Institute, and what could they possibly gain from experimenting on Turnips? Neurodivergents, I could understand, but Turnips? They were just normal people living their lives. It made no sense.

I set the video in the night's evaluation queue to see if a more in-depth analysis could help me reach any conclusions, but the only thing it gave me was a headache. Frustrated with my mind, and all the unanswered questions, I hurried through classes. Maybe if I could find a good time to find Steele and break into Martial Academy's server room, I could see if they had any information on the Institute—or on the Company's Director.

By the first Martial period that morning, I'd decided to use Ms. Graff's habit of sending me off for errands to go find Steele. Unfortunately, she wasn't accommodating and I found myself sparring with Hunt again. She was upset about something, and working faster than she usually did. It took most of my attention to keep up as she lashed out at my head. I grunted as Hunt got inside my defense and delivered a half power blow to my temple. The world flashed with stars, but she didn't stop. I triggered the BYE-BYE module to clear away the distracting thoughts, then tied the PREP module in. I barely intercepted the next strike, and it was a good thing I had. Even with a proper block, the skin of my forearm stung as she pulled back then went in for another strike.

I refocused on the clash-separate-clash rhythm of the exercise. It was a 360° drill we'd been doing since the first time I'd joined Mr. West's class, so it was nearly automatic. But nearly automatic wasn't automatic enough.

I could hear Ms. Graff yelling over the labored breathing and grunts of an exercise-in-progress about working slowly; adjusting to our partner's ability; practicing hard, but safely. Hunt obviously hadn't heard any of it. We were running at almost six times the speed as all the other groups, but I was working with a Prefect, so no one said anything. Graff just ignored us.

I staggered back as Hunt tried something that wasn't in the drill and it connected with the side of my jaw. I got my hands back up, ready for her to come in again, but Hunt just shook her head with disgust. *No wonder you got beat up by Houston so bad,* she thought. Aloud, she said, "Keep your mind on the fight or you're really going to get clobbered."

I snorted. "Ms. Graff was just telling us to work slowly. I'm new at this, remember?"

"That was slow. It was also right outside your comfort zone. Well, deal with it. We aren't all nice happy teddy bears who want to give you a hug. If you can't remember that, then you're going to get killed." *And dead isn't the same as a little bit alive. They won't be able to bring you back this time.*

I bit down hard on a retort and went to get a drink from my water bottle on the edge of the mat. When I looked back at Hunt, she was over with Ms. Graff. The two were talking with their faces away so I couldn't read their lips. After a moment, Hunt started back toward me.

"Come on. Let's try the drill again," she said and led me back toward the space we'd claimed on the mat.

She'd squared up and was just about to start the round when Ms. Graff stiffened. I caught an unfamiliar stream of thoughts come and then leave her mind. Someone had just projected a message to her—and they hadn't been careful about it. Still, speed had made up for secrecy. I couldn't intercept any of the messages. Ms. Graff turned to Hunt. "Something just came up. You've got the class." Then she left.

"Yes, ma'am." Hunt frowned at me, and I started examining her thoughts more closely.

Alright Farina, I know you're listening. It's a bad habit, but useful right now.

My eyebrows rose. Hunt was a Company operative. Why would she be directly communicating with the enemy? I revised that thought as soon as I had it. The Company wasn't our enemy—no matter what Ms. Green said.

I need some help from someone like you.

I stiffened. She wanted help? Just because the Company wasn't my enemy didn't mean that Ms. King wouldn't come down hard on me just for thinking about helping her.

Relax. It's not directly Company related. Look around. What do you see?

I scanned the room, but nothing seemed to be out of the ordinary.

Where's Briggs?

I looked around again, but he wasn't there. Actually, he hadn't been here all day. I remembered how terrified he'd been, talking to Hunt last week.

::What happened to him?::

Hunt shook her head. *I don't know. The Company flagged him as a possible kidnapping target—not for us to kidnap, understand, but someone has been taking Turnips off the street. Mostly military types or bullies like Houston. I was supposed to watch him. He never came in for classes this morning. No one else seems to notice. Ms. Graff just said she hasn't even heard of him. Someone's messed with an awful lot of memories to make him disappear, and we don't have the intel to find him.*

I balled my fists as I saw Briggs's face in my memory. The image faded as an unfamiliar program came into play, redirecting me away from his current whereabouts. I wiped the program away, and a dozen notifications flooded into my mind. Briggs was missing!

I clenched my teeth. I knew something was wrong! Why hadn't I dug into his mind to figure it out, sooner? If I had, maybe I could have protected him.

Hey, don't blame yourself. These people are sneaky. We had our telepaths go over him, but they couldn't find anything. The Institute—the people we think have him—is very good at mental manipulation.

::What do you want from me?:: I asked, silently.

Just talk to Smith. She knows I work for the other team, so we don't exactly get along. Also, keep an eye out. I've heard a rumor from the top that the Agency's picked up some important things that might shed a light on this whole situation. You don't have to tell me if you figure something out—I work for the Company, after all—but do me a favor and tell Medina? He'll know what to do with the information. He's paranoid, sure, but he's not a bad sort.

How did Hunt know about Medina? I started to ask, then stopped. Did it really matter?

::I'll see what I can find out.::

Hunt smiled. *Thanks, Farina. Now I think something else has happened. Something big, or Graff wouldn't have left like that. You should probably get downstairs.*

Then, aloud she said, "It looks like we don't have even numbers anymore. Farina, you're going to run an errand for me."

Downstairs. Hunt clearly wanted me to go down to the Agency base, and was giving me an excuse to do it. But why? I dove past Hunt's surface thoughts and sifted through her mind. The answer was well hidden, but present. She was a double agent. She might be working with Ms. Graff, but she was also feeding Medina information. How had the Company Projectors missed that? Had they even thought to look? The Company was less choosy about who they allowed in their ranks, which was how they'd ended up with Houston. Did that mean they weren't looking for Agency spies?

Regardless, I had the information I needed. I pulled out, nodded to Hunt, and left.

Smith met me as I turned down the hallway. "Farina, there's an emergency meeting for all tac officers and analysts downstairs." Then she paused. "I was supposed to get you from class. How did you know?"

I started to answer, only to stop. Ms. King said that one of the most difficult situations an agent could be in was working for two different sides at the same time. Spreading Hunt's status as a double agent around would make her job nearly impossible. But Smith was waiting for an answer.

"Ms. Graff left suddenly. I figured I might be needed."

Smith closed her eyes a moment, then she smiled. "So the Social History class has been good for you."

I nodded. Between laser tag games, we spent most of our time talking about what was acceptable in what cultures, and how to navigate certain circumstances. How to lie to cover a friend's six was one of those circumstances. There had also been a few lessons on seduction, poisons, blackmail, and everything in between.

Smith turned and hurried off. A few minutes later, we followed the stream of people through the rotunda and into a sort of lecture hall.

Medina, Ms. King, and Ms. Green all sat at the front of the room, facing rows of seats stuffed full of tactical black, lab coat white, and the casual dress of Analysis and Admin. There were representatives of every single department here. Hunt was right. Something big had just happened.

Ms. Green placed a small, sticky dot the size of an ant on her throat and called for everyone's attention. Her voice reverberated around the room, and I smiled. That thing on her throat was a mic I'd seen while working in R&D. It was one of the technologies set to go on the civilian market in a few years as it bore little military use. Except for times like this, apparently.

"Now, I'm sure you're all wondering what's going on." Her voice was crisp and clear as it rang through the room. Some of the tactical officers nodded their heads. "We received notice that all Company operatives were just recalled from their patrols and that the few that *have* gone out have been in forty-agent squads."

Now some of the analysts were nodding. They'd probably seen this info come across their desks.

"Then, roughly twenty minutes ago, they called on their reserves to go active."

That brought a collective hiss. Why would the Company call on their reserves? Obviously they thought they needed the extra brain-power. Was there really something that could pose that much of a threat to a neurodivergent organization? Were they preparing to declare war? Whatever the reason, I didn't like where this was going.

Ms. Green's eyes swept the room. "Consider this a warning, especially you going out in the field. Though InDep is refining what little data we have, we don't know much about what the Company is up to. As of right now, we are at General Alert 3. For those of you who haven't been here long—and there are a few of you," she looked at Smith and I, "General Alert 3 means that you are to be ready to be called to both external and internal operations at a moment's notice. Anyone authorized to have a weapon is to be armed at all times." Her voice deepened in seriousness. "This is not a step we take lightly. Watch yourselves, and report anything suspicious directly to your superiors. Now, if you'll direct your eyes to the screen, Director Medina has some intel he'd like to share."

Ms. Green returned to her seat as everyone's curiosity spiked. Medina accepted the dot-mic and started up a display with the standard deployment of Company teams we were used to observing. He outlined the changes in firepower and the technological advancements we'd observed—including the new mind shields. I tuned out the buzz of noise and focused on Ms. King and Ms. Green's reactions to all this. Doubtless, they'd heard it before. Ms. Green's face was unreadable, but Ms. King's face held something almost predatory. She wasn't worried. No, it almost looked like she was…waiting?

Medina finished the briefing and dismissed the crowd. We filtered back through the door, and I stopped at my locker to retrieve my duty weapon. Briefly, I wondered what would happen if I had to use it on a Company operative. Briggs would tell me to decide now that I would do whatever I needed in order to protect myself and my team, but I couldn't. I'd seen what horrible people the Company employed, and I'd seen what damage they could do—but I still wasn't convinced that the Company was evil. They were desperate.

Could I bring myself to shoot someone whose only crime was desperation? I dismissed the thought as quickly as it had come. I could cross that bridge when, or if, I came to it.

CHAPTER FOURTEEN

I got transferred to Ms. King's advanced Krav Maga class the next day, and spent half my time working with a 'guest instructor' named Neal Black. After that, I got detention twice. Once from Ms. King, and once from Vera Hunt. When I presented myself at Ms. King's door that weekend, Black was the one to open it.

"Come on," he said, jerking his head toward the door that led into the game area and then to the Agency below the school. "Ms. King wants me to work on your combat. Sounds like she wants to turn you into a real Hitter."

I frowned. That was the one Tac job I wanted the least. I could handle being the projector telepath for the team, and I could enjoy being their analyst, but that thing with Houston was a fluke. It was a tactical *team* for a reason, and Tolden made sure we knew it. I wouldn't be sent down solo again and we already had Black and Tolden as hitters. We didn't need a third.

When I told Black that, he spun around and looked me straight in the eyes.

"That might be how an Intel team is set up, but Flex teams like us don't have the leisure of manipulating the situation so only the people who should be in the line of fire are. We take the situation as it is. Sometimes that means getting sent in solo while the rest of the team sets up, and I don't plan on carrying you into the chopper again. Got it?"

So we worked for two days straight at everything a hitter needed to know. As the weekend progressed, Black got steadily grimmer.

Finally, I stopped. "What's wrong?"

He looked up from polishing his gun and then jerked his head at the targets down the range. "More bullet holes, less talking."

I safetied the gun and set it down on the table. "Something is bothering you, Black. It has been all week."

He just grunted and went back to his gun while I waited. Seven minutes later, he still hadn't responded.

I started to pick up the gun to go back to the shooting exercise when Black finally slammed the last piece of his weapon back into place and sighed. "You ever get the feeling that someplace is too quiet?"

I nodded.

"Tac 47 hasn't been called out all week—not even for a cursory Intel scan. The last time that happened was 9-11. Something's in the works now, but I have no idea what. Tolden's worried too, and Steele—if he would pay any attention."

"And that's why this extended training session?"

He snorted. "Kid, this ain't no extended training session. You've barely scratched the surface. Put that thing away and follow me."

We went back out, but instead of going to my locker so I could put my gun down we turned into the armory. My blue lines went wild, and I gasped.

Hung on the walls in neat rows were weapons with sleek silver casings and the tell-tale flare at the end.

"Those are plasma weapons," I said.

Black's eyes narrowed. "You ever seen one in action?"

I shook my head. "Only in simulations."

"And where would you have seen a simulation?"

I tapped my head and then whistled as I started getting the energy outputs readings off them. "I tried to build one, but decided to make the plasma pulser instead. It's a little less deadly. I never could figure out how to get over the efficiency wall with either device, though. These have to be running at seventy-six percent efficiency at least."

Black snorted. "Twenty discharges per cartridge, point-eight second recharge time, and a range to rival a standard firearm."

So that was how they got around the recharge time I had on my pulser. A cartridge of pressurized, concentrated gas from which to draw would keep the weapon from having to pull it from the surroundings.

"How long have you had these?" I asked.

"As long as I've been around," Black responded and ventured farther into the room. "Here's one you'll admire," he said and pointed to a wall where the casings had a similar design, but without the flare. There was something about the cartridges—

I blinked as the blue lines spit out an answer. "Electrical weapons? This is what you were talking about in D.C.."

He nodded. "Quick, dirty, and mostly survivable. Lets you shoot first, ask questions later. As of the Alert 3 announcement yesterday, everyone who's certified is carrying one."

I squinted at them, but my blue lines didn't have the background information to provide much more data. "Can I try it?" That way I'd be able to get more complete specs.

"Tolden said to certify you when he found out you've got a contact discharge version in the works. Grab one and let's go."

The energy pistol had dismal range—barely larger than the range on my plasma pulser—and only two charges per cartridge. I stored the information in my mind, and pointed the muzzle down range. I squeezed the trigger, expecting a little recoil and some sort of boom. The thing tried to jump out of my hand, and only the training I'd had in the last few weeks stopped me from dropping it. I started to turn to comment on the excess recoil, then stopped as my blue lines spit out energy discharge specifications. If someone caught a full blast to the head, they'd end up in a coma.

I pulled the trigger a second time and re-checked the numbers. They were correct. I slammed the gun back down and turned on Black. "That's not mostly survivable—that's everything-except-dead! If someone gets hit in the head with one of these blasts, it's going to take years to recover, if they recover at all!"

Was this really what the Agency used to go after people they weren't even sure were criminals?

Black grinned. "That's why we've got pods. Mostly dead is still a little bit alive, and that's all the pods need to work with. Just think about what shape you were in when we got back from the mission with Houston. It would have been a long road to recovery without those pods but you were back to combat within the day."

"And if one of the pods fails?"

I looked back at the electrical weapon. This thing was nothing like the glove I was working on. This was designed to fry most of the neural network in the human body.

"If the pods fail, then we have worse problems than one prisoner in a coma. Our line of work is dangerous, and the medics rely on those pods to wake up anybody we bring back half dead. That said, we've got three of them, so there is some redundancy."

My eyes widened. "Only three? Why not make more?"

What if someone came in and all three pods were full?

"We can't. We found them in an abandoned lab thirty years ago. Occasionally, a new R&D type tries to reverse engineer them. We've gotten a few useful technologies—like the bio-cards—from those attempts, but nothing near the level of the pods."

I frowned as he motioned to the electrical weapon again.

"Break-time's over. You wanted to work with the electrical weapons, so work with them."

I grit my teeth and picked the weapon back up. It wasn't much better than a bullet to the brain, but it was progress. Plus, the data I got from these weapons would help me make a better version of the electropulser.

CHAPTER FIFTEEN

Smith had been crying. I could see the redness around her eyes when I sat down next to her for lunch. My blue lines spat out a reasonable explanation: she knew Briggs was gone.

::We'll find him, Smith,:: I projected to her.

She stiffened. *How are you going to do that when he doesn't even want to be found?*

::Doesn't want to—:: I reviewed the conversation I'd overheard between Hunt and Briggs. He almost certainly wanted to be found.

He's on some sort of Military training mission.

::And he left without telling anyone?::

You know what it's like, working with a school like this. He couldn't exactly spread it around. His class might not be as secretive as ours is, but they don't advertise.

And a training session wouldn't inspire so much terror—or make him start working with Hunt. Something else was going on here, and the numbers suggested that it might be the same 'something else' that had the Agency and the Company at each other's throats. What was it Ms. Graff had called it? The Institute?

I'd heard that name before, but where?

A few fuzzy memories flashed over my vision, but they didn't leave me any wiser. Except—the only other times these memories had surfaced were while I was looking at Superiors, and every one of them was at the Agency, both from my first visit, and just after I had told Medina what I'd found at the D.C. overflow facility. What could possibly make me forget, or even blur, something I'd seen?

A headache cracked over my skull, and I groaned.

"What's wrong, Farina?" Smith asked.

I waved her off as I finally put the pieces together. It was obvious, now. Someone had placed a strong set of suggestions in my mind and blurred my memories. Once, because I'd seen something they didn't want me to see, and a second time because I had almost figured something out. I archived that information and set a timer for them to resurface, just in case there was another set of compulsions set to keep me from pushing through the first layer, then tried to shake off the headache. I could work through all that data later, but I only had so long I could talk with Smith.

"I'll be fine." Then, ::Briggs has been acting strange, lately, right?::

Smith nodded. *It's textbook sulking, though. He wanted to tell me about his new training assignment, and he couldn't so he was sad. Now he's gone without even a goodbye. I understand it, but that doesn't make it hurt any less.*

Except, according to Vera Hunt, he wasn't on a training mission. I couldn't exactly tell Smith that without blowing Hunt's cover as a double agent. But that did bring up an interesting question. ::If he couldn't say anything about the training mission, then who told you?::

She looked up. *He went missing this morning. I didn't think anything of it until the Agency's announcement yesterday. When I told Ms. King I was worried about him, she checked the military's database for me. I thought something worse might have happened. Sometimes people just disappear, you know, and they might be in trouble. Plus, there are those Superiors who are taking people—like the prisoners they abducted from D.C.. I don't know what I would do if they had taken him.*

I choked on my food. Was Ms. King was involved in this mess? My odds of keeping my investigation for Hunt secret just plummeted. But Ms. King had to know that Hunt was a double agent, she was the Agency's recruiter! Was she also investigating how to get Briggs back? That would explain the misdirection. Ms. King was buying herself time to investigate by feeding Smith a believable lie—which meant she probably wouldn't be very happy I was meddling in it. Still, why didn't Ms. King trust Smith with the investigation? Smith was a full agent, and had far more training than I did. We were both on one of the Agency's most prestigious tactical teams!

No, Smith had a right to know. Briggs was her friend, too.

I clenched my jaw and tried to figure out how to deliver the news, but there wasn't really a good way, so I just told her. ::Briggs isn't on a training mission. He's been taken by some bad people.::

Smith hissed. "What are you talking about? Ms. King said he was fine." She bit her lip as we drew looks from the students around us at the lunch table.

::I don't know what Ms. King was thinking, but Briggs is anything but fine. I felt some of his thoughts spill past his walls earlier, and he is terrified of someone. I don't know who, but I'm going to try to figure it out. I'm going to need some help with that, though. Has he been going anywhere different than usual? Staying at school more? When did he start getting distracted?::

I compiled the information as Smith gave it to me, growing more grim by the second. She was convinced the Superiors had taken him. I wanted to argue, but as I sorted through recent footage of him, I could see changes in his physical form. They were slight enough I hadn't noticed it, but a full analysis showed it all. He was taller, with denser muscles in strange places. Upon closer inspection, I could find puncture marks in his arm that matched the syringe marks I'd seen in the base in D.C.. The Company was right. The Institute was taking Turnips and turning them into Superiors.

So why hadn't they just made Briggs disappear? Why let him return here, and risk him asking for help? I didn't have answers for those questions, and Smith couldn't think of a single place where he might have met someone from the Institute. Still, I had more information than I'd started with.

I wrestled with the potential models during my next academic period, but couldn't make much headway until an alert began to flash in the corner of my vision.

Fix the tampering? What—

The memories flashed again, and my headache returned. It was definitely a good thing I'd set that alert, because something had made me forget all about the memories that had been tampered with.

The models of Briggs could wait. Whoever had messed with my mind was going to regret it when I fixed what they'd done to me. I dove deep into my own mind, like I was going to my safe space, except I never entered that room. Instead, I found the deep storage vault where I kept all of my memories. I set my blue lines to work finding scenes with blurred faces or mental frequencies that didn't shift with my thoughts. The first time was over a semester ago after Robbins had finished vetting my memories. I had been convinced that he hadn't messed with anything. I clenched my jaw and watched the memory through. Sure enough, there was a notification there telling me that something was off, but the medical teleprojector had wiped it away with a gentler touch than I could ever hope to achieve.

I found the compulsion he'd grown into the fabric of my mind and ripped it out. The memory sharpened until I could even hear the words he spoke. The sounds were strange in my mind, so I moved on. I did *not* want to think about the implications of that right now.

The next memory was of the Superior woman I'd encountered

when Tolden first brought me to the Agency, and the things I'd found in her head as I escorted her from the rotunda to her cell. Her face, the models I'd built, the conversation we'd had—all of it was covered in a web of compulsion and forgetfulness. No wonder I got a headache every time I tried to pull all the data I had on Superiors to the front of my mind. I had sort through, dismiss, and then fight free of this mess every time I did it!

I set to work dismantling the strings piece by sticky piece— only when I shifted one thread, the others started growing to fix the hole! After twenty minutes of playing whack-a-mole with the web, I snarled and jerked the whole thing free. This was my mind, and Robbins couldn't mess with it!

Suddenly, I was inside the memory. The Superior woman stared at me with muted horror.

I am not an Instructor, I am a defect to be corrected or thrown away. Just like you neurodivergents, and the rest of humanity. They will not stop until they have created the perfect Superior—their perfect soldier. Not human, but better than human.

This was the Institute the Company was chasing—and the Instructors were doing genetic experiments on people like Briggs. The Agency had a Superior in InDep, and Ms. Green had still walked out of that meeting? They had proof of what the Institute was doing in their own Intelligence department! And Medina? He had seen this Superior with his own eyes when I helped transport it to his department last semester. They were deliberately turning a blind eye to this. Was that what the Superior woman had meant when she asked if I was just going to go along with the Agency's machine?

I curled my fingers into fists. No. I was going to go down there and get some answers. Then I was going to find what- ever place the Institute was hiding Briggs, I was going to tear it down, and then I was going to bring him back so Smith wouldn't be sad anymore.

I was going to protect the people I cared about. Otherwise, what was the point of being a Projector?

CHAPTER SIXTEEN

That weekend, I woke up early to go down to the wing of Interrogation where I remembered dropping the Superior woman off. I scanned the memory for any signs I could use, and hoped my clearance would hold. The elevator didn't have a problem with my card, and neither did any of the doors between the rotunda and the desk that blocked the interrogation portion of InDep from the rest of the department.

The agent at the desk was in full tactical gear—and so was I. Ms. King said that the best way to get somewhere you weren't supposed to be was to look like you belonged there. I figured that a tactical agent in full gear would be waved past faster than a kid in street clothes.

I nodded to the agent at the desk, who was staring intently at the computer. His thoughts revealed that he was playing Pac-Man. I suppressed a snort and waited for him to run into a jelly. Finally, he looked up. "Tac's down the other elevator, hon." He tapped the key to start a new game.

I clenched my fists at my side. The last person to call me 'hon' had ended up under a car. ::Actually, I'm Agent 32. Not 'hon'.:: I projected.

He jumped to his feet, away from the computer as he realized his mistake. There were only five projection telepaths assigned to this base, and only three were on-site at a time. One was a PS1, and the other was Robbins, an old hand. The other two were assigned to Strike teams, so they were cycled in and out—and none of them had a Tac 47 patch on their tactical suit. From his thoughts, I could tell that stories about me had gotten around.

"U-uh, what can I do for you, Agent?" He started to salute,

then aborted it and settled for standing at attention.

Just like that, the anger rising in my mind turned to humor. I projected a thread of assurance. "I've been told there's a prisoner who's requested to speak to me."

"Uh, ma'am? I don't see anything like that in the system." His wariness skyrocketed, and I took a moment to smooth the edge off. I was going to have to be careful with how much coercion I applied. The Agency didn't look kindly on Projectors using their abilities to get into places they shouldn't.

I tried again. "The prisoner is in room twenty-four."

He looked at me, then back down at the computer. He typed in something, then blinked. "That's strange. It's requesting a security code." He typed in a few digits. "It doesn't look like I'm cleared for this information." He reversed the screen and handed the keyboard over.

Big red letters covered the screen, "Access Denied". I tapped in my code, and the screen changed.

"Report to Director Medina immediately."

I swallowed. So much for that plan. The agent looked at the screen, and pointed down the hall the other way. His other hand was on the firearm on his belt. "I'll escort you there."

My stomach twisted as I followed the tac agent down the hall. I ran as much analysis as I could on Medina's past behavior, hoping it would give me some insight on how he would take this little venture once he found out, but there wasn't anything conclusive. Medina was a hard man to read.

The tac agent opened the door to Medina's office, and I stepped inside. The director motioned to the chair on the other side of his desk without looking up from his tablet. After a long moment, he set it down with a sigh.

"You've been busy, Agent. R&D has nothing but praise for your work, AnAd has spent the last two days trying to recreate the analysis you did in two minutes, Tactical can't figure out how you've become proficient in every commonly used firearm they have, and now I find you trying to access a prisoner you should know nothing about."

A chill ran down my spine as I reached for his surface thoughts, only to find a cold hard wall. Medina was as unreadable as a chunk of ice. I marshaled my blue lines to map out the possible consequences of the line of reasoning he'd just laid out, only to swallow hard.

There were very few people who could accomplish the list of tasks he'd just described—and most of them were spies who weren't learning those skills, but who already had them. Suddenly, I regretted trying to get in there to talk to the Superior. I'd charged in without thinking because I'd been blinded by a need to help Briggs.

"I only recently found Robbins's tampering, sir. Now I have questions."

Medina arched an eyebrow. "Completely understandable, except for one piece. How could you tell it was Robbins?"

"My lines tried to warn me right after he messed with my thoughts. He wiped that from my awareness at the time, then buried the memory. Once I started looking, I found the alert."

Medina grinned. "That's a useful trick. I'll let him know. He's usually good about that sort of thing, but we haven't run into very many Visuals like you. Actually, I don't think we've ever seen anyone like you, Miss Farina."

I blinked. "You knew Robbins was going to mess with my memory?"

"We don't know very much about the Superiors. In fact, we know far less than we should, given the circumstances. The fewer people who know about them, the better control we have over when that information becomes Agency-wide, and the fewer people are prematurely assassinated. Trust me, we did you a favor."

Assassinated? I couldn't tell if it was a threat or not, given the matter-of-fact expression on his face.

"So what happens now?" I asked.

"What do you want to have happen?"

I bit my lip. Medina kept turning this back on me, like I could answer his questions—like he was being reasonable. This was just a way for him to give me enough rope to hang myself with. I closed my mouth and leaned back in the chair. I'd already charged in without thinking once. I wasn't going to make that mistake again.

Medina sighed. "Agent 32, that wasn't a rhetorical question. Do you want to keep digging into the Institute? Do you want out of the Agency? Do you want to go back to being a regular tactical agent? Your options are open. I just want to know where you want to go from here."

I stayed silent—though I did trigger the WATCH module. It sent my lines into an analysis frenzy so I could see the slightest twitch of a muscle and, now, the merest hint of an unguarded thought. The downside was that I couldn't keep it up for long without tiring myself out.

His eyelids twitched as he watched me sit there motionless, then his eye flicked down to the left corner of his vision, and he frowned. That move was deliberate—and practiced. His muscles moved in perfect synch, and then stayed where he told them to go. Medina must be a fantastic poker player.

"Look, Farina, I'm trying to help you here. I can't do that if you refuse to work with me. Now, Robbins is outside. If you want to play this way then fine. I'll call him in, and we can get this over with."

"You can't wipe my memories," I said. I tried to keep the sounds even like I was practicing in Ms. King's class but I couldn't tell whether or not I was successful.

Medina inclined his head. "Can or can't isn't the question here. I don't bluff. That doesn't mean I want to wipe your memories and expel you from the Agency. I have a feeling that would get very messy for everyone by the time we were through. Instead, why don't you tell me why you wanted to talk with the Superior?"

This wasn't any less dangerous territory but, if what Medina said was true, I didn't have much of a choice.

"A friend of mine has gone missing, and I think the Institute is involved. The Superior talked to me last time, so I figured that asking her wouldn't be any worse than asking the Agency—who is apparently under the impression that Briggs is on a military training mission."

"I see you've been talking with Hunt, then. Good. I don't have a problem with you interviewing the prisoner so long as you show me the memory through my interface device and promise not to talk about her existence to anyone. That includes Agents Smith and Hunt. Understand that even the strike team that brought her in has had their memories altered. Very few people know of her existence, and even fewer remember that they know."

I couldn't decide whether to be pleased that Medina had given in so easily, or worried about what he was going to do after I reported my conversation to him. The man was a complete enigma. Still, his terms made sense, and at least it would put me on that list of people who knew about the Superior.

I stood. "Thank you, sir."

He followed suit and extended a hand, which I took. "Do think about what you want to do in the future, Agent. There isn't a department in the Agency that wouldn't snap you up in a heartbeat—and mine is no exception."

"I will." I turned to leave.

"Oh, Agent Farina?"

I looked at him back over my shoulder so I could watch his lips as he spoke.

"I will expect to see you here immediately after your interview with the prisoner. Be prompt."

I nodded and hurried away.

The tac agent from before led me to the Superior's room, and let me inside. Then he locked the door after me. I barely noticed the lock turn, though. All my attention was on the woman sitting in the chair. Her eyes were closed, back ramrod straight, with hands cuffed to the table.

"You've changed," she said with her eyes still closed.

I pulled a chair from the corner of the room and sat across the table from the Superior. "Yes, you could say that." After all, quite a bit had happened since the last time we'd met. Now I knew who and what I was. I wasn't scared of my own shadow anymore.

"You are not easy to find," she said.

I cocked my head. "Yeah?"

Her face twisted into a slight smile, eyes still closed. "You left no name for me to call you by."

"Neither did you."

She was faintly amused. "They just call me Defect. I'm the only one with Instructor genes that isn't Psionic. I prefer just D."

"I'm Crystal Farina, Agent 32."

Her eyes snapped open. "I guess that was unpreventable. I warned you about merely going along with the Agency's machine." She shook her head. "They read your mind, I suppose.

Pity. They surely know where I am by now."

"They?"

"The Institute. I told you before. I am a failed experiment—too smart by half to be a Zeta-Superior, and without the mental abilities of an Instructor. My walls make me hard to control, and now, by coming to you, I've completely broken my training. Oh yes, they will kill me the moment the Instructor they've sent to be your watchdog finally gets up the courage to unsheathe her claws."

"Claws?" I looked at her hands, but they looked perfectly normal. The Superiors in D.C. had two inches of white bone where their nails should have been.

D bared her teeth. A moment later, razor sharp claws were jutting from her fingertips. "A natural weapon. They are long enough to kill, hard to detect, and quick to deploy. What other natural weapon would the Institute give their Superiors?"

I swallowed. "They're trying to create super soldiers? Why?"

She looked at me through slit eyes. "You're the perfect little neurodivergent, figure it out. And while you're at it, why don't you figure out why I'm talking to you instead of your Intelligence Director?"

"You want me because I'm new."

She grinned, showing a mouth full of teeth that could cut through bone. "And because you're independent enough to do what needs to be done. The Institute has been steering the Agency to places it could be useful but out of the way for years. Sometimes through donors. Other times, though more direct means."

My blue lines spat out the logical conclusion to her explanation. "You think the Agency has someone from the Institute inside it, guiding what we do."

"Yes. That person has been looking for me since I got here,

but she has been blocked by your little friend. As soon as she gets clearance from the Institute, he won't be a problem anymore, and I'll be an example." Fear; icy and cold flashed through her consciousness in spite of the nonchalance in her surface thoughts. The disparity between the layers of her mind was impressive. She had more control over her thoughts than anyone I'd ever seen. What had driven her to develop that control?

I brushed that question away. It wasn't the most important thing right now. "You must have things you want to accomplish? If the Institute was not coming for you, what would you do?"

That brought her to laugh—but it was a twisted humor that stemmed from painful memories deep in her mind. "I want the Institute to burn, and then I want to leap into the flames and dance on the charcoaled corpses of the scientists who created me."

I flinched away from the savage joy that slashed across the layers of her consciousness as fire lit in her eyes. I definitely did not want to continue down that road. I changed the subject again. "You still haven't answered my question about why the Institute is creating super soldiers."

"No, I suppose I haven't. I didn't think it would be hard to guess, though. They're taking Turnips and turning them into Zeta-Superiors capable of kidnapping fully trained neurodivergents to experiment on. When their process of creating Alpha-Superiors—fully Psionic war machines like the Instructors, but without the gene pool problem—is complete, they will be able to evolve the rest of humanity so that they, also, are Superior."

Evolve the rest of humanity? "They want to change us? Why?"

She gave a derisive snort. "They throw around words like 'curing cancer' and 'ending death', but they really just want a population they can control. Toppling regimes is difficult, but promising everlasting life with powers most Turnips only dream of makes it that much simpler. They argue that this is merely an extension of what nature is already doing. You neurodivergents came about naturally, after all. They are merely speeding up the process. That's one of the reasons they needed an individual to penetrate your organization. The fact that she's in a perfect position to make me an example to any Superior who dares disobey them is only a perk."

"And who is this Instructor you think has infiltrated the Agency?"

She shook her head. "You wouldn't believe me if I told you, *Agent*. She is in the perfect position to deceive any new additions to the Agency. Even if you did believe me, you wouldn't be able to defeat her. She's a PS8, and an E100,000. That means she can lift over half a ton with her mind alone—understand? You would have to go after her by yourself. In short, you would never survive."

I clenched my jaw. D wasn't wrong. I had never heard of a Psionic with so much raw power at her disposal. Still, I'd come here to try and find Briggs, and whoever this Instructor was, she would know where he was. I had to try. "Who is she?"

D closed her eyes. "You would call her Ms. King."

"What?" I stood, and the chair behind me fell over. "You have to be mistaken. I've been watching her, and she couldn't possibly be—"

I snapped my mouth shut as the blue lines flashed for attention. I let them take me back through my memory and watch every time Ms. King stared out at me with that predatory look in her eyes. Mr. West had warned me that someone in the Agency wasn't who they claimed. Now, who was the person he'd had the most contact with? Who was in the best position to figure out that he knew, then manipulate Houston into eliminating him? Who had shifted my mission during the fundraiser when it looked like I was going to discover the man with the badly tied bowtie was a Zeta-Superior?

Ms. King was there for all of it, posing as the one person I could trust to guide me through my transition to the Agency. Well, at least I knew how she'd controlled the Superiors that had tried to attack me a few weeks ago. She was an Instructor, and that was her job: to instruct the dumb little super soldiers her makers had created to do their bidding. She was a general in the Institute's army, and they'd been using her to keep the Agency off their tail.

Taking her down would be just as impossible as D feared. I wouldn't just be fighting Ms. King. I would be going against the entire Agency.

That brought another question. What in the world was I going to tell Medina?

"You see it, then."

I nodded as the Tac guy from the front opened the door. "Are you alright?" he asked. "The sensors picked up an impact."

That would be the chair. "I'm fine. Tell Medina I'll be out shortly. I have his answers."

I looked back at the Superior sitting there with a battleground instead of a mind. She was telling the truth, and it was her last hope. I could see the fate that waited for her through the fractures of her mind as she tried to keep it together. They would breed her for her genes, and then take her apart piece by piece.

I shuddered. No one deserved that. "I'll do the best I can," I promised, and then I left—still racking my brain for what I was going to tell Medina. There was no guarantee he would believe me, even if I told him the truth. If he believed me, great. If he didn't, he had the resources to make sure I never left InDep again at best. At worst, he would warn Ms. King, and even my blue lines couldn't calculate what would happen then.

My phone buzzed, and I bit down a curse. What now?

Steele's secure messaging app held a message from Tolden. "Scramble."

I looked at the Tac guy standing between me and the door and said the only phrase that could hold Medina off. "I'm on Tac 47, and we're deploying."

His eyes widened. "I thought 45 and 46 were on call today."

"Tell that to my Agent In Charge," I called as I jogged past him. He let me go, and a few moments later I was on the helipad waiting for the others. The Tac guy in InDep wasn't wrong. Tactical 47 had been on call two weeks ago. Tac 45 and 46 should be handling this call unless there was something that gave us the edge or they were already called out.

CHAPTER SEVENTEEN

Tolden's face was pale when he reached the chopper. He was scanning the mission brief on the tablet in his hand while he jogged—something only a telepath would dare try. He rammed the tablet back into its holder and swung into the chopper.

"What's going on?" I asked.

He finished jamming his harness closed. "Just get in the chopper. We lift as soon as Steele gets here to pilot."

I did as I was told, but I broke protocol enough to scan his mind as he finished reading the briefing. Maybe one day I would break the habit of just taking whatever information I needed from the minds of others, but Tolden was a big boy. If he got annoyed that I was using my abilities to effectively read over his shoulder, he would tell me. As it was, he stayed silent and I got the gist of the mission.

A Superior was in the middle of attacking a civilian population in Millennium Park. Tac 45 and 46 were handling similar calls, and Tac 47 was going in because I had a record of success against them. Also, unlike the on-call Strike teams, we didn't have any injured team members. Seventy percent of the strike teams that operated out of Martial Base had at least one member in MedDep right now.

Black, Smith, and Steele catapulted into the chopper and secured their straps just moments after Tolden had finished reading the briefing. The chopper lifted as he started talking.

"You all know we've been tracking the Company's new deployment patterns. The places they are responding to are linked to sightings of the same creatures we fought at the base in D.C.. We're still not sure what these Superiors are, or even if controlling them is in our ballpark, so we've been trying to hang back a little. Ladies and gentlemen, that just changed. Five minutes ago, Ms. Green issued a directive allowing us to take down any Superiors who might endanger civilians or draw attention to the neurodivergent world. This directive came in response to a wave of Superior attacks against civilian populations. We don't know what the situation looks like on the ground, and we still don't have a good grasp of Superior capabilities. We're dropping fast and hard. Black, you're in front with me. Smith, you're on Turnip duty. Get them out of the line of fire. When that's done, you're on analysis. Don't let the thing touch you—you find what high ground you can and try to get a bead on it. If you get a clear shot, you are authorized to take it. These things are fast, and it's better to drag in one dead Superior than a dozen dead civilians. Steele will be providing air support if we need it."

To Black's bloodthirsty grin, he said, "Only if we need it. Understand? We're trying to keep these things out of the public eye, and a missile strike in Millenium Park won't help. Farina, your job is to subdue the thing mentally—or at least distract it."

"Drop point is in sixty seconds," Steele warned. "We have civilian and police Turnips on the ground."

Tolden cursed. "Get the police forces out of the way. If they get killed trying to intervene, Ms. Green is going to have my head. Farina, can you lay a heavy compulsion on them? Get them to retreat?"

I nodded. Laying a compulsion on a neurodivergent was difficult because they knew it was possible. Turnips wouldn't know what hit them.

"Drop point in twenty seconds," Steele said.

Black snapped out of his harness and pulled a box from under his seat. He tossed me a gun and a glove. A quick check revealed that the gun was a plasma pistol. The glove was a prototype electric weapon I'd been working on. I'd adjusted it to make use of similar paths the electric weapons in the armory used, except to run through a Superior's nervous system. It would stun a human just fine, but it would drop a Superior for a week. Hopefully.

I didn't have time to ask where he'd gotten the glove. I just pulled it on, shoved the plasma pistol into an extra holster, and grabbed the rope as Tolden hauled the chopper door open.

"Go, go, go!"

I dropped out of the helicopter and slid safely to the ground. Smith, Black, and Tolden landed around me. The policemen didn't seem to see us as they fired wildly at the creature bearing down on them or, if they did, they were too crazed by fear to stop shooting.

"Superior at eight o'clock!" Black warned, and we all scattered.

Bullets buzzed past our heads as the line of policemen fired at the Superior—not that their shots did much good. Blood trickled down the side of its torn blue t-shirt in six places I could see. The bullet lodged in its calf should have reduced it to a sobbing mess on the ground, but it moved effortlessly through the bushes—trailing broken sticks. A moment later, it was inside the stand of trees the cops were using for cover. I blocked out their screams as best I could and started toward them. They couldn't deal with this monster. My blue lines started a side comparison, but it was shoved into the background as I triggered the BYE-BYE module. I needed all my lines working on task if I was going to avoid getting shot by the terrified men with guns on the other side of the park.

"Farina, get those Turnips out of here! Smith, we've got civilians in the line of fire. Get them moving!" Tolden shouted. My blue lines marked places where civilians that couldn't make it into the clogged train access were cowering behind trees and bushes at the edge of the park. Near the street, shops doors were being barricaded—stranding everyone else outside.

I danced out of the Superior's way as Tolden caught its attention with a double tap to its center of mass. It tried to charge through me, claws swinging to try and get me out of the way—like I was an obstacle, more than a threat. I started to plot a course to try and intercept it. If that thing reached Tolden, he would be in big trouble. Then my blue lines froze. An alert flashed on my vision, and my blood ran cold.

"Briggs?"

My blue lines overlaid Briggs's face on the Superior's and I gasped. Eighty-nine-point-six percent match. I pulled on the WATCH module to drive my lines faster. Time slowed as the Superior wheeled around. I ran another analysis, this time taking the oddities in the Superior's physical form into account. Ninety-nine-point-six percent match.

The Institute hadn't just taken Briggs. They'd turned him into a Superior.

"Briggs!" I screamed at it, but there was no recognition in those eyes as it bounded toward Black. I grit my teeth and focused my attention on the creature that had once been my friend. There had to be something of him left. If I could bring that remnant to the forefront, he would stop long enough for us to sedate him. There were projectors back at the Agency that could recover his mind, if only I could find some inkling of the Briggs I knew. I needed to save him!

I planted my feet into the ground and dove into its mind. There! I gasped as I found the memory center. It was empty. The only thing powering this beast was a single, pitiful video. A black haired Instructor with cutting emerald eyes and teeth like razors stood in front of him and detailed this mission.

He was to find a public place and feed on the pathetic masses until special agents showed up. Then he was to kill them and return to the place where he'd been made. An image of my face flitted through his mind, and the Instructor growled. *"This one is to be brought back alive. Kill the others."*

I could feel his hunger to please the Instructor, and his thirst for blood. I searched through the rest of his mind for anything that remotely resembled the friend I'd known— some recognition that *I* was one of the people he'd been sent to subdue—but the only things I could find were memories of his satisfaction as his claws ripped into human flesh. He didn't know I was his friend. He didn't even know what a friend was. I clenched my fists and kept looking. There had to be a way to fix this. I had to turn him back! I'd already failed him once. I had to save him now!

I grabbed at his mind, sifting through every crevice that could possibly be hiding my friend. There was nothing. The Briggs I knew had died the moment the Institute had kidnapped him. They had re-made his body into this thing that relished blood, destruction, and pain—even the pain of bullets grinding between his bones as he moved. This thing wasn't Briggs. It only wore his face.

I clawed my way back into my own mind and scrambled for cover.

"What's going on, Farina? Where are you on the police?"

Police? I took one breath, then another to regain my focus. I tried desperately not to think of Tabitha's reaction when she found out.

A thought, like a scream, split the air. I wheeled around to look at Tolden.

::Smith needs help.:: From someone who understood what it was to lose a friend.

He nodded. "I'll go. You get those police out of the way."

The Superior had finally figured out that we were the agents he was supposed to kill. He left the corpse of the police officer he'd torn apart, and turned, licking the blood from his lips. His eyes froze on me, and I wondered if he'd yet recognized me from the image the Instructor had shown him.

I took a step back, and it fixed its gaze on my abdomen. Desire, far more potent than Houston's had ever had been, wafted from his mind at the thoughts of all the delicious intestines I had crammed inside my belly. We'd officially been upgraded from annoying obstacles, to food. The Instructor's directions were secondary to bloodlust. A moment later, it was almost on top of me—moving faster than anything I'd ever seen! My odds of survival flashed at two-point-six percent.

Black bowled into the Superior from the side, snagging its attention. "Come here, doggie."

Superior occupied for a moment, I focused on the policemen. They were out of their minds with fear, discharging their weapons as rapidly as they could under the misguided assumption that rate of fire could make up for the difference in biology. I gathered my strength and *pushed*. It didn't take much added hysteria to make them drop their weapons and run. Soon the bullets had stopped flying.

I turned to evaluate the situation, only to find the Superior bearing down on me again, galloping across the mud churned grass on all fours. Black's distraction hadn't lasted long—the Superior obviously knew there was something different about me. I pulled the plasma gun and fired. The discharge only skimmed the Superior, which was just enough to make it mad. I fired again, but it rolled under the shot without missing a stride. I dropped to the ground and slid under its claws, firing up the underside of its belly as I went. It snarled and leaped away as the shirt melted into its bubbling skin. Underneath it all, I could see my blue lines straining to keep my emotions in check. I had to remember that, as much as this creature looked like Briggs, it was the thing that had killed him. It was beyond human emotion. The Instructors had modified it so far that it was only a monster. I could kill a monster, if it meant that fewer civilians suffered the same fate Briggs had.

"Farina, you alright?" Tolden asked. I nodded and reached out to his surface thoughts. His words had drawn the Superior's attention. He started sprinting away—but no one could outrun a Superior. "Black!"

"Got it." Black came in from the side again. Of all of us, Black had the best chance of emerging alive from a hand-to-hand encounter with the Superior—and he'd proven his ability to redirect the creature for a few moments.

Smith is back in the chopper, Tolden thought. *She said something about this Superior being a friend from school? Do we need to turn this into a strictly recovery mission?*

::It might be his body, but they ripped his mind out and replaced it with that.:: I motioned at the Superior as it got down on all fours again so it could make use of its long, hairy forearms as it charged. It wheeled around as sirens and lights caught its attention. It was going after the fleeing police vehicles.

I pushed the info to Black and Tolden.

"I've got it." Black snarled and went off in pursuit.

Tolden triggered his com unit. "Steele, keep eyes on Black. He's going to try and turn that thing around."

I turned back to Tolden. ::We're going to need a head shot to take this thing down. I can try to disrupt its neural function with my electropulser.::

Tolden nodded, and ran a practiced finger over his weaponry. "Then here's the plan." He triggered the com unit again.

"Black, drive it toward us."

There was a grunt on the other side of the line. "I hope you've got a step two. It's coming in hot."

Tolden frowned. "Farina, you get in there the moment this thing gets back. Let Black take the heat if you can, but get past his mental walls and slow him down. I'll cover you. If you can get it to stop moving long enough, I can take it out."

That meant I would have to be close—close enough to watch the light leave those eyes that still looked remarkably like the Briggs I knew. I clenched my jaw, and thought instead of the bodies that littered the trees. This wasn't a Company operative following orders. This was a monster that deserved to die. I grunted acknowledgement of the plan.

Five seconds, kid, Black warned. My blue lines flashed as it calculated the Superior's speed. It was coming in too fast! There was no way for me to engage unless I could slow it down. I dodged out of its way as it tried to lock its fangs around my arm. A civilian shrieked, and the Superior barreled toward the noise, spurred on by sounds of helpless prey. I discharged the gun and missed. I pulled the trigger again, but nothing happened. The charge was gone. I dropped the useless energy weapon and focused on the thing's mind— only to slide off invisible walls. The poking around I had done earlier must have triggered the crystal shield. I spotted the device controlling his shield strapped to its neck like a collar on an attack dog.

::It's shielded—I can't get through.:: If these were the same mechanical walls the other Zeta-Superiors were using, this was going to be more difficult that I'd thought.

Tolden grunted. *So the Institute can learn.*

The Superior sank its claws into the civilian's arm, just below the shoulder and lifted her up so her feet scrabbled for purchase. It tilted its head, drinking in her helpless terror.

"No, please!" she screamed. Tears dripped down her cheeks. "I have a son. You don't want to—" Her begs turned to gurgles as the Superior closed its empty hand around her throat and ripped it out. He tossed her to the side like a used rag and stuffed the handful of meat and bone into his mouth.

Tolden swore. "This area was supposed to be clear!"

I scanned the area again as Tolden moved to engage the Superior. Fury burned the edges of his mind.

::It's clear now,:: I reported, and shoved the guilt away. There was no time for that. If we didn't take this thing out now, more defenseless civilians would die.

Tolden grunted as the Superior slashed at him. *Go find cover. We'll drive it close to you. Let's see if that electro pulser is as good as your plasma pulser was.*

::Keep it as slow as you can,:: I said. ::I need direct contact with its head.::

The Superior got its claws around Tolden's arm, and I could feel the flash of pain scrape across his thoughts a moment before he got it under control. *Slow, fast. I don't care. Just take it out!* He freed himself with a tug that sent blood running down his arm, but he barely noticed it as he drove his fist into the Superior's jaw.

I found a bench a little ways down and signalled that I was in position. Even through its shields, I could feel the bloodthirsty creature coming toward me. A moment later, the blue lines in my vision turned purple and I boosted over the bench. I pushed off the smooth wooden surface one more time and tucked to complete the rotation. The fingers of my free hand dug into its hair to stabilize me as I used my legs pin its deadly claws against its own body. My blue lines flashed a prompt. This was the moment I'd been waiting for!

I slapped my palm against the back of the thing's head. My pulser was turned all the way up. It jerked once and spun, trying to throw me off. I held on for a moment, but it twisted savagely. My grip on its scalp shattered. We were face to face, and I no longer had the upper hand. It drove its claws into my shoulder and flung me to the ground. My blue lines erupted into warnings. The Superior was above me. It's teeth brushed my throat—

It shuddered, then collapsed on top of me. Hot blood ran over my forehead, and into my eyes and mouth. I spat it free and shoved it off me. When my eyes were clear of the blood, I examined the corpse. There was a hole the size of my thumb straight through its skull. An analysis on the bullet—lodged in a tree trunk beside me—flashed in my vision. Who on the team was armed with FMJ rounds?

I pulled the visuals, then blinked as I saw Smith with a sniper rifle.

I expanded myself to try and find Smith's mind. Tolden had said she was in the chopper with Steele, and sure enough, she was. My eyebrows rose in surprise. She'd made that shot from a helicopter in flight? Even with my analysis tools, that would have been impossible. The vibrations from the chopper, mixed with the differing air waves—the girl was a wonder.

I could feel the satisfaction mixing with grief and guilt inside her mind as she collapsed into tears. Briggs was really gone.

I wasn't fast enough to save him.

But why? Evidently, there were people in the Agency tracking Superior movements. I wouldn't be surprised if Ms. Green knew exactly where Briggs had come from. But the lies Ms. King had been feeding her meant that the Agency hadn't acted until it was too late. Now my friend was dead.

Ms. King had to pay.

I grit my teeth and reached out to Tolden's mind. He was inside the stand of trees the Police officers had been using for cover. I could feel the constant lap of pain from his scored arm as he checked something in a bush.

I jogged up to him, trying to figure out how to break the news about Ms. King. His gift must have picked up some of my budding anxiety, because he stood and turned to look at me.

I clenched my jaw. ::I have something to ask you, but it will be simpler if I share a memory with you first.::

He gave me a strange look. "Sure."

I pulled the memory of my last conversation with D and projected it to him.

He jerked as if struck. "Are you absolutely certain she was telling the truth?" he asked.

I nodded, and my head felt like lead. "If I wasn't, I wouldn't have come to you. I'm putting together a team—we don't have much more time." If this wasn't set up by my next Social History class, Ms. King would read my mind and figure out that her cover was blown.

Tolden stared at me with disbelief—and rightfully so. What I was asking him to do would mean his job, at the very least. But I needed help. I couldn't take on Ms. King alone, and I couldn't go back into her classroom without her figuring out what I knew. Then I would be really, really dead.

"Even if you're right, what you're asking us to do would be nearly impossible, not to mention suicide!"

"I'm not asking the team to do anything. I'm asking you because I trust you," I responded. Then, after a quick scan to make sure there weren't any unaffiliated telepaths in range, I slowly dismantled my shields. "You're a telepath, read my mind. My shields are down; take any information you want."

Tolden frowned. "I believe you're telling the truth, but it's still a serious risk. Taking down a PS8 is nearly impossible without a massive amount of set up, and taking down someone who's off the charts in telekinetic endurance is nearly as hard. Someone who happens to be both at the same time, and some sort of super Superior? Well, you saw how hard it was to take that thing down." He motioned towards the helicopter. "You won't be able to do it with just my help."

I nodded. "I know that. But I don't have another choice."

He didn't react—almost as if he'd anticipated my response. Maybe he had. My shields were still down, after all. I took a moment to rebuild them. While I had no illusions as to what would happen after the operation, I wanted to keep my job until I could take King down. Letting that information out unguarded wouldn't help with that goal. "So?" I asked quietly.

"I'm in—but only if you extend the offer to the entire team," he said.

I released a breath I hadn't realized I was holding. "It's a deal."

I turned to look at Black, who was jogging up to us.

"Look, you can chitchat in the chopper, but Ms. Green says she wants an update STAT." Black jerked a thumb back at where Steele were finishing securing the Superior's dead body.

"We're coming," Tolden said. "Start up the chopper."

CHAPTER EIGHTEEN

Smith stared at the Superior's body the whole way home with tears in her eyes. I could barely look at it, though. When I saw it, all I could think of was how I'd almost put the pieces together once, but Robbins—no, Medina—had stopped me. If I could have figured it out a few hours earlier, I could have saved him. Now he was dead.

Finally, Smith closed her eyes. "How could this happen? How could Briggs have turned into one of these monsters?"

I brushed her mind to find guilt turning into anger. I looked at Tolden, who nodded. If I was going to ask Tac 47 for help, now was the time.

"There's an organization called the Institute. They're conducting experiments that turn Turnips into Superiors. They're the ones the Company has been tracking, who blew up our base in D.C., and who planted the bomb in the hotel."

Black's eyes darkened. "How do you know, newbie?"

"Because I pay attention," I snapped. "The Agency has been looking the other way. They've been suppressing our memories whenever we meet these Superiors while they run around blindly trying to figure out what to do."

"The Agency can't do that," Steele said. "I would have seen the data come across our systems in CIS."

"Did you see a data spike since I joined the team?"

His voice on the com went quiet for a moment while he sorted through some information in his own mind. "Yeah, but we've been tracking more Company activities since around then."

I shook my head. "No. That's the analysts in AnAd trying to break down the model I gave them of the Superiors from the very first time I saw one. You'll find a similar spike from after our mission in D.C.."

"If they've known about Superiors for this long, why haven't they said anything? Surely Ms. Green doesn't condone the Institute's activities?" Smith said.

"Because Ms. King is one of Ms. Green's closest advisors, and she'd been running interference. I don't know everything she's been doing, but I do know this. She is an Instructor for the Institute, and she told you Briggs was on a training assignment with the Military so you wouldn't start looking for him.

Smith clenched her fists. "That is the last mistake she'll ever make."

I could feel her thoughts shifting with Black's. They were going to march into Ms. Green's office and demand she send a team after Ms. King—but Ms. Green wasn't going to listen to them any better than she'd listened to the Director of the Company.

"Do you really think Ms. Green is going to listen to you?" I projected clips from Ms. Green's meeting with the Company into their minds. "She's seen all the same things I have, but Ms. King has blinded her. The Agency won't wake up enough to fight these things until Ms. King is gone."

"That's insane," Black said.

"Is there another choice?" Tolden asked.

The chopper was silent except for the constant *thwap* of the rotor blades.

Tolden sighed. "That's what I thought. You don't have to get involved with this, if you don't want, but you saw what one Superior did back there. If the Institute is really building an army of these things, we need to be able to respond. Every single one of you is on Tac 47 because you are flexible. You can change targets whenever the mission requires it—well, our mission has changed."

Smith folded her arms like she was giving herself a hug. "Ms. King is going to pay for what she did to Briggs. I'm with Crystal, with or without you."

"Do I get my chair is CIS back if I do this?" Steele asked.

Tolden grinned. "If we survive, and then stay out of prison—sure."

Black shook his head. "You're all going to get yourselves killed."

"Maybe," Tolden said, "but this is what we do."

"Then you're going to need someone who can handle a plasma cannon."

I made my way to the InDep elevator as soon as Steele set the chopper down. Tolden knew where I was going, and had assured me that he would mount a rescue operation if Medina was somehow in on Ms. King's plot. When the door to InDep opened, Medina was leaning against the opposite wall, cleaning his fingernails. I noted a spot of blood on the arm of his usually pristine white shirt.

"Prompt, huh?"

My blue lines presented me with an image of Medina from the last time we'd spoken. He'd reminded me to come talk to him immediately after I'd interviewed the Superior. He'd also been wearing the same exact shirt—minus the blood.

"Given the circumstances, I think I did pretty well to get here at all," I said. "What happened to you?"

He looked pointedly at the scratches the Superior had left on my arm. "She didn't give you that, did she?" She? He must be talking about D.

"No. That's from the thing we were deployed to take down. Now stop ignoring the question."

"It looks like you were successful in your mission. Good." He clapped once, then stood. "Now, I think you promised me some intel?"

I grit my teeth and followed him into the safety of his office. He placed the interface device on his desk, then looked at me expectantly.

I folded my arms and matched his gaze. "What happened to you?"

He lifted his eyebrows. "To me? I think you ought to be far more worried about that shoulder of yours."

"Yes, but you're going to get a mission report that tells you exactly what happened to my shoulder. Where did the blood on your shirt come from?"

The right side of his mouth lifted. "Occupational hazard, I'm afraid. One doesn't take my job without being prepared to defend oneself from assassination attempts. Don't worry, it's his blood—not mine. Now, the intel you promised?" He gestured to the interface device.

I frowned. The timing on Medina's assassination attempt was interesting. I wondered if Ms. King had felt threatened by him and tried to resolve the issue while most of the Agency was busy dealing with the Superior attacks around the city. I bit my lip. If that was the case, perhaps he wasn't working with Ms. King and my caution was unnecessary. Still, it wouldn't be that hard to put a spot of blood on a white shirt. He could be lying to try and make me trust him.

I stored the analysis with a shrug. There wasn't really any way to tell, one way or the other until I saw his reaction to D's information. "You're not going to like what you see," I said.

"Undoubtedly." He motioned to the interface device.

I placed my hand on it and went back to the interview I'd had with D. Medina's face revealed nothing as he watched, and he didn't so much as twitch when the Superior named Ms. King as the spy. My throat went dry.

He already knew.

I cut the scene and locked the PREP module into place—just in case.

"Well, thank you for your assistance Agent Farina. You've been invaluable." He pushed away from his desk. "I have some things to attend to. Do be careful on your way out. Also, I would avoid Ms. King for the foreseeable future. It would be unfortunate if she discovered her cover was blown, don't you think?"

I didn't move. Was he working with Ms. King, or not? Was he going to go warn her, or assemble a strike team? I couldn't tell, and my mind bounced off his like a rubber ball off concrete. Hunt said he was trustworthy, but she was one of his agents. Of course she thought that.

"Is there a problem, 32?"

I frowned. "Am I going to meet Robbins on my way back down to the rotunda, sir?"

He spread his hands in front of him. "I don't see any reason why you should. He's assigned to Medical."

"He's assigned to you."

Medina smiled. "Perhaps, and perhaps not. I am not in the habit of discussing my agents. If it will make you feel better, I can call Medical and ask what he's doing right now."

I bit the inside of my lip as more analysis overlaid my vision. D had been in custody for over a semester, and she was still alive. Why was that? If Medina was working with the Institute, she would have been dead weeks ago. He had to have been running interference so that Ms. King couldn't be completely sure that we even had the Superior—which was why he'd had Robbins erase those memories. If I had gone back to Ms. King's class worried about the non-human creature I'd just helped escort to a holding cell, Ms. King would have known exactly where to find D.

I still couldn't be completely sure. There were a dozen factors that could explain his behavior—but this was my best shot.

"Director Medina, how long have you suspected Ms. King?"

He sighed. "It's my job to be paranoid, to compartmentalize information and to control all the factors I can."

Which was about as straight an answer as I could get out of him right now. I grit my teeth. "She knows you suspect her, so she'll be watching you. You'll never get a Strike team set up in time—not with her abilities."

His eyes hardened. "I'm listening."

"I've told Tac 47 about the situation, and they've agreed to help. We're going to go take down Ms. King as soon as I get back from briefing you."

Medina's lips thinned. "You weren't planning on telling me this, were you?"

I shook my head. "The Agency's been compromised. I'd be a fool to think Ms. King is working completely alone."

Medina sat back in his chair to think for a moment. Then, "Tactical 47 wouldn't have been able to take Ms. King down even before they lost their last Teleprojector. You need help."

"The moment we brief a Strike team, Ms. King is going to know."

"Then don't use a team from the Agency."

I hissed. "The Company isn't too happy with us right now."

The corner of his mouth tilted up. "Yes, but what do you have to lose?"

Everything. Last semester, I'd finally found a place where I belonged. I was doing some real good in the world—helping people! If I went through with this, I could lose all of it.

Medina was suddenly leaning on his desk, eyes locked on mine. "If you don't want to go through with this, then don't. I'll call Robbins up here right now, and you can go home. I will handle the rest of you team, and there won't be any risk of you alerting Ms. King. If you want to take her down, though, you need allies. Now there is a critical difference between friends and allies. Friends are people you trust to help you, whatever the circumstances. The Company and the Agency will never be friends. Allies need to have a gun, and be pointing it the right way. We share a common enemy with the Company, 32. They may not like it, but they will help."

I could see Mr. West's face overlaid on my vision. He would have bent the heavens if it meant taking down Ms. King.

"Fine. I'll talk to them. We need to move fast, though. Even with the element of surprise, Ms. King is going to be hard to defeat."

Medina nodded. "That she is, but I think Cal can probably help with that. I borrowed her for a little side project after I heard that the Institute was experimenting with neurodivergents. She has a very interesting device down there."

I stood and reached out to Steele's mind. He was already down in R&D, checking some things, so it wouldn't be out of his way to pick up Cal's little device.

"Thank you, sir," I said, and meant it.

Medina gave me a little smile. "Don't thank me yet, 32. You've got a long way to go."

My knuckles halted just inches from the door. I swallowed, and forced myself to knock. If this were Mr. West, asking for help would be easy. But he wasn't here anymore. He'd figured out Ms. King's little secret, so she'd had him killed.

A few moments later, the door was open and Ms. Graff was staring at me. "What do you want?"

I opened my mouth, then closed it again without making a sound. "We might want to go into your office."

Ms. Graff's wariness skyrocketed as she readied herself for an attack. Still, she stepped gingerly out of the doorway and motioned for me to precede her.

I thanked her and led the way to the sliding mirror that had once served as Mr. West's office. I stopped next to the picture frame, and plucked off the camera I'd installed earlier. Ms. King did not need to see me voluntarily meeting with Ms. Graff. A few moments later, the teacher was seated across from me.

"Now, what do you want?" Her body language showed no hint of the violence readying inside her mind, but I was monitoring her thoughts as closely as I could without taking my attention completely away from the situation.

"As you know, I work for the Agency, and you work for the Company—so let's not play games."

She stiffened. "You're a telepath."

I tilted my head. "I'm a Projector Telepath, Elaine. There's not a lot in your head I don't know." I swayed out of the way as a 'decorative' knife came off the back wall and whizzed past my ear. "I haven't come to expose or kill you, but we have a mutual problem."

The next knife stopped behind me, and I could feel Ms. Graff considering her options. Killing me would be messy, and escalate the conflict between the two organizations, which the Company couldn't really afford if it was going to focus on the Institute. Letting me live when I posed such a security threat might bring her superiors down on her. Apparently her Director was not a very forgiving man.

I held up a hand. "Just let me speak. If you reject my proposition, then I leave and neither of us know any more—or any less—than we knew before."

If anything, she stiffened further. "What's your strength rating?"

"That's not relevant unless you continue your attack. Otherwise, you find out first hand." My voice was cold, and the blue lines in my vision monitored the teacher's every breath as she considered the threat.

"Fine." The knife lowered slowly to the ground, but I had no doubts about her ability to bring it up as fast or faster than I could get out of the way. Telekinetics with Ms. Graff's endurance rating were nothing to mess around with. Still, this insanely powerful telekinetic had just agreed to at least listen, so I took a deep breath.

"Thank you. Now, the Agency recently gained custody of a Superior. I'm sure the Company already knows of their existence, so let's skip the pretenses."

Ms. Graff's eyes narrowed. "Yes, let's."

"Well, she has alerted a very select number of people within the Agency," well, one person, "that the Institute has infiltrated Martial Academy."

She leaned back into her chair. "The Company has long suspected that a third party has infiltrated the military and is currently teaching here. I assume this is the person you're talking about."

"Yes, only the party infiltrating is called the Institute, and the party infiltrated is the Agency." I let that sink in, feeling the wheels turning in Elaine's head.

"Who's the teacher?" she asked, lips pursed.

"Ms. King."

There was a moment of shock, then she grit her teeth. "That wasn't the name I was expecting. She's a what? A PS8?"

"Yes. And an E100,000."

Ms. Graff sat forward abruptly. "That's impossible. It's twice the height of the scale we use. I could practice my whole life and not even come close."

I nodded. "That's because you've only ever measured humans. She's a genetic cross between the Zeta-Superiors we've been seeing, and a very powerful neurodivergent. I don't know all the details, but apparently, she's a precursor to what the Institute thinks is the next evolutionary step of the human race."

Ms. Graff nodded. "Yeah, we've known about Superiors for a while now—and we've heard whispers of what the Instructors can do. I just didn't know Ms. King was one of them. That would certainly explain the spike we saw in Institute activity." She was still processing that Ms. King—instead of being the public face of the Agency—was actually a killing machine, but there wasn't enough time. I needed her help now.

"Look. I'm putting together a team to take her down. Are you in, or not? I've seen the Superiors in action, first hand, and you obviously know what they can do, too, or you wouldn't be sending out forty person teams."

She looked up from her whirling thoughts. "How do I know you're telling the truth?"

I pursed my lips. "Did you hear about the fiasco in D.C.?"

"200-plus personnel taken down by an unknown party. Base was blown up to cover. That's about all our intel got."

Of course that was what they would have seen—the same way we saw them trying to plant a bomb in a building just downtown when they had really been there to diffuse it—same as us. But the time for convenient fantasies was over. They hadn't planted that bomb, the same way we hadn't blown up our own base.

"You're partially right. There were 200 personnel. The party that killed them was the Institute. The Agency still hasn't sorted through enough of the rubble to figure out what the official story is, but I was on the tac team that found that mess. The bomb was a trojan horse designed to explode in the infirmary of the containment facility a few blocks away, not a cover-up. My team and I barely escaped the two Superiors sent down to investigate what went wrong.

Her eyes widened. "You escaped pursuit by two Superiors with a team of, what? Five people?"

I nodded. "You can't take Ms. King down alone, and neither can I. But I think we can pull it off if we work together."

I closed my eyes and monitored Graff's thoughts carefully. This was the point of decision. She could either accept the offer, or reject it and attack. I wasn't stupid—I knew that I'd handed the Company intel they'd gladly kill for, and I'd identified myself as a Projector with enough power to erase memories. That was more than enough to justify a bright red target on my back.

Finally, she nodded. "If you're taking down the Institute, we're all in."

CHAPTER NINETEEN

I grasped the handle and suppressed my racing thoughts. If I entered this room, there would be no more hiding and no more pretending. What I'd already done was enough to get me locked up—giving classified information to the Company was an unthinkable offense—no matter that Medina had suggested it. But assaulting the Agency's recruiter? My team and I might not live long enough to celebrate the thousands of lives we'd saved. Unfortunately, Ms. King would kill us all the moment she saw even a glimpse of this in our thoughts. There really was no choice.

I'd already gathered my team, and they were all waiting on the inside of the door. Those people all knew the danger and were willing to accept it. I could do no less.

I twisted the handle and slipped inside Ms. Graff's classroom. Tolden, Black, Steele, and Smith all sat against the right wall, hands on their weapons, eyes locked on Hunt and Ms. Graff who were on the other side of the room.

"Farina. Good, you're here. Tell these trained monkeys that there's no reason to worry. We're not about to shoot *them* in the back," Graff said. Her thoughts were scathing, but she was probably the calmest in the room. She was leaning against the wall, whistling silently as she tried to keep her anger under control.

"Monkeys? Who are you calling monkeys!" Black leaped to his feet, and the tension ratcheted up another notch as Elaine's weapon appeared in her hand. Tolden's mirrored it, and suddenly the entire room was armed except me.

"Not another step. Just because we aren't going to shoot you first doesn't mean you'll offer us the same courtesy." This was from Vera Hunt, who was kneeling behind an old fashioned semi-automatic.

I stepped between them before Tolden could finish forming his response.

"No one is going to shoot anyone," I said. "Black, Tolden lower your weapons." If they put their guns away, the rest of the team would follow suit.

Black glowered at me. "You don't get to give me orders, Farina."

I shrugged. "Well, if someone doesn't give ground somewhere, I'm going to get filled with a lot of holes. So, if this petty feud is more important than taking down the Institute, then go ahead." I turned and caught his gaze as I spread my arms wide. "But neither organization reaches the other unless it's through me."

Are you sure they're on our side? Tolden asked silently.

::What side?:: I responded. ::They're all human, and that's the only side that matters right now.:: I didn't tell him that Hunt was actually working for Medina. I was about to break a dozen Agency rules, but outing Hunt was not going to be among them.

He nodded, then holstered his gun. "Lower your weapons."

I could feel Black's indecision as Steele and Smith holstered their guns. "Farina, they don't intend us any harm?"

I nodded.

The Company's weapons dropped.

Black snorted and shoved his gun into the holster strapped to his thigh. "Let's hope your gift is still as impressive as it was when we went after Houston. It might be the last day of my life either way. I'm in."

I turned to Elaine Graff. "You've briefed Hunt?"

She nodded.

"That's much appreciated." Then, turning to Steele, "You got the device I sent you for?"

The curiosity in the room spiked as Steele nodded and produced a square box with two knobs—almost like a pair of handles. He tossed it to me so I could inspect it.

"Cal seemed pretty shocked when I asked for it," he said.

I turned it over to let my lines get a better look. A few moments later, my blue lines spat out the device's function and I nodded. "According to Medina, telekinetic abilities—like teleprojection—are multiplicative." I brushed away a stray image of the group of PS1 projectors at the fundraiser. "The problem is actually interfacing the two sets of abilities. Any gaps, and suddenly it's just two people pulling on the same object. This is supposed to help make that interfacing easier. Our best intel puts Ms. King as an E 100,000 and, if I'm not mistaken, we have an E800 and an E300 here."

Black's jaw stiffened as I mentioned his telekinetic abilities. "You aren't putting me on the sidelines, Farina. No way."

Ms. Graff held up a hand. "Even if we can interface our abilities, it's not that simple. We're going to have to figure out where Ms. King is focusing her telekinetic power, and then work together to push against it. We won't be able to do that until whatever object she's using starts to move, and someone with that much ability will have the target object where she wants it before we can even start to push against it."

I decided to ignore Black's objection for the time being. "That's where Tolden comes in. Once I get her shields down, he'll be able to get inside her head and tell you where to go. Meanwhile, Hunt and I will try to keep her busy, while Smith covers us." There were nods around the room, so I took a deep breath. "We're only going to get one shot at this. Let's make it count."

"Miss Farina, would you please stay a moment?" Ms. King's voice was worried, so I reinforced my shields again. As much as I'd tried to subdue the feelings of betrayal that surged every time I looked at her, I couldn't be sure nothing had leaked through. She still stood tall, with sharp eyes and a sharper tongue—looking exactly like the teacher who had guided me through learning to control my gift, and sent Mom a new couch to replace the one Smith had bled on. Except now I knew her secret.

It was hard to reconcile the image I saw in front of me with the vision of Briggs down on all fours, bleeding from a dozen bullet holes as he charged us mindlessly. Had Ms. King been modified like the Superiors? Like D?

Sure, she was tall, and perhaps her forearms were slightly longer than average—but she certainly didn't look inhuman. She looked like my teacher.

"Of course, Ms. King." I realized I'd been quiet for a fraction of a second too long, and tried to recover by keeping my voice as light as possible while the other girls filed out the door. I'd made it through the entire class without tripping any of Ms. King's alarms—that I could tell, anyway. We were too close to mess it up now. Using the cover of the table, I pulled the electropulser glove on. It had stunned the last Superior long enough for Tabitha to get a shot off. Hopefully it would work this time, too. I didn't have a gun—it would be too much of a risk. We'd been instructed by Ms. Green to carry weaponry everywhere, but Ms. King had made it clear after the declaration that those who were full agents could put their weapons in the cubbies underneath the counter during class time. That meant there was no way for me to remain armed during class without Ms. King figuring out that something was wrong—which might just provide the incentive she needed to look past my surface thoughts and tear down my mental walls.

"Are you feeling alright?" Ms. King asked. Her face was twisted into a concerned mask, but her eyes shone. She suspected something was wrong.

I mentally checked Tolden's position. He was almost there—and hopefully the others were too. Tabitha was circling around to Ms. King's office. Tolden and Black were at the door to the arena. Ms. Graff was waiting with Hunt in the hallway. I resisted the urge to wipe the sweat from my forehead.

"Yes, why?" I asked Ms. King.

"You've been asking tense, is all. I wanted to make sure everything was fine. If the Agency's been giving you problems—"

Tolden reached the door, and I crumpled to the floor in a maneuver we'd practiced in Social History a dozen times. I flipped the switch on the electropulser, and grabbed Ms. King's face as she tried to catch me.

The teacher started convulsing as the electricity tore through her body.

"Now!" I shouted, and Tolden dove into Ms. King's mind. I followed, seizing control of the centers in her brain that controlled her gift, and smashing down her walls.

Then there was an impact that tore me out of her mind and sent me spinning into my own body, only to groan. Blood trickled down the side of my head, into my eyes. I wiped it away.

"Where's the Defect?" Ms. King roared.

I picked myself off the floor as Hunt charged.

"You're never going to get her."

Ms. King whirled, batting Hunt out of the way and coming around to stare at her office. I could feel her reaching out to the weapons in the cubby where I'd put my gun at the beginning of class.

::Got it?:: I asked Tolden. He nodded and started shouting directions to Black and Ms. Graff who were holding the box between them.

I watched as the concentration on Ms. King's face increased. Sweat dribbled down her face, but she was far from done.

"You!" The Instructor pointed at the team of three busy thwarting her efforts.

I felt the disturbance before I saw it. A crackle of energy in the woman's finger. The blue lines flashed red on the box that linked the telekinetics—but there wasn't time to warn them. If that box got broken, we would all be dead!

I dove between them to catch the blast on my shoulder. The force propelled me backward and my face smashed into the floor again.

I brought the blue lines in my vision back to life and assessed my injury. The adrenaline pumping through my system kept me from feeling the full brunt of the pain. My nose was broken from the impact, and my shoulder wouldn't hold pressure well, but the blast hadn't hit anything life threatening. I jumped to my feet and scanned the room again. None of the telekinetics had been hit, and Ms. King was still playing with them, even as she was busy taking Hunt apart. Smith joined the fight as Ms. King smashed Hunt out of the way and charged towards Tolden and the others.

::Smith, get out of there! She'll kill you.::

But she didn't even acknowledge I was there.

I tried again. ::This isn't helping Briggs. Go grab a weapon and try to get a clean shot. That's where you can do the most good.::

I stepped into the fight next to her, and pulled her out of the way of Ms. King's claws. I dropped her on the ground and pulled the WATCH module. Every blue line I had was assessing her, plotting intercepts and avoidances, watching for patterns in her mind that would tell me what she was trying to do.

I put my brain on autopilot while I dove into the Instructor's mind once more. It wasn't easy this time—the walls were almost back up far enough to keep me out, but I was determined. Hunt rejoined us, then got knocked back out. I altered the pattern to compensate as I smashed Ms. King's walls down for a third time.

::Tolden?:: I sent a tendril of thought to his mind to make sure he could get back inside Ms. King's mental defenses, but his mind was full of thought shards drifting outside of a fractured mind—overshadowed by agony. He was hurt bad.

I redoubled my efforts, wrestling for control of Ms. King's entire body. The battle came to a standstill. My eyes were locked on hers, and she was locked on mine. Then my concentration lapsed, and I was fighting for control of my own body.

I tasted blood as I bit my tongue, but that didn't really matter. I threw up wall after wall to protect the inner core of my mind. I shifted frequencies until I'd cycled through more colors than I'd seen in my lifetime. I wasn't looking through my eyes anymore. Not really. But then there was a flicker in my vision and that changed. My walls came down as I saw the *face* in my vision.

I stumbled back, hypnotized by the familiar lines and curves of the man that suddenly, incomprehensibly appeared.

"Daddy?" The whisper was quiet. Raw, and full of anguish. I could see his face—the black stubble below his lip. The scar on his cheek. The curve of his chin.

The walls of my mind shot back up, and Ms. King was gone.

It was the face. The face I could never remember. I stared into his golden eyes and delicately placed the image where it belonged in my memory. The room around me faded to a charcoal grey, completely unimportant now as the man in front of me shrank—or maybe I grew. He was still taller than I was by two inches as he stood there with his back to me. I wasn't a child anymore. Somehow this wasn't a memory. I stood in the greyed out husk of my childhood living room with my father in front of me, and every moment was real.

He turned.

The black hair framed his tanned face. His nose was just slightly crooked, and his eyes were the shape of almonds. And gold. Very gold. He had black fuzz on his chin from not shaving, and his cheeks were thin and drawn. The scar that ran from his eye to his cheekbone was still raw—maybe two weeks old. What had happened to him?

"Why?" The breath escaped my lips before I could snatch it back. "Why did you leave?" The sounds echoed in my ear, crisp and clear like a bell. This was the sound of my voice. It was different from the voice I remembered hearing as a child. I was older now.

He didn't answer. He just stared at me with mournful eyes.

"Did you know I was different? Did you know I was a telepath?"

He still said nothing.

"Tell me!" I couldn't keep it in any longer. I screamed the words. My hands were fisted at my side. I wanted to cross the gap and pound his shoulder with my fist. I wanted to grab him in a hug and never let go. I wanted him to come home! I never wanted to see him again. Instead, I just stood there, staring at him.

He looked back at me with the answer in his eyes. ::Yes.::

The grey world shredded itself, and I smashed into the hard wooden floor of Ms. King's classroom. My eyes snapped open and I looked around. Everything was different. Colorful. Panic set in at these unfamiliar surroundings as I wiped the wetness from my cheeks. Gasps and moans filled the air around me, tearing at my heart. Who were these people littered on the ground like broken dolls? Where did he go? Where was Dad?

A woman with a blistered face struggled on the ground against something or someone I couldn't get a clear look at. The blistered woman was between us, growling to herself—or at her opponent. The sound of bone sinking into flesh passed my ear, followed by a gasping gurgle. No one else was here—or, not anyone awake. Bodies littered the floor, unconscious but alive.

I met the green slit eyes of a cat staring at me from across the room as the woman with the blistered face turned her attention back to me. The person—a human woman—she had been struggling with was dead behind her. Her throat was ripped open even as she still gasped for air. The woman with the blistered face had blood smeared on her arm and chest from where the arterial spurt of blood had drenched her. No, that was wrong. This woman with the blistered face had a strangely shaped mind. It wasn't a *she*. It was different.

I looked up at the *thing* as it rose to its feet. A smile curled on its face. It expected me to fear it—I could tell that much. But what was fear? Why would I be afraid? A cold smile settled on my face.

::What are you?:: I asked.

It stopped and looked around.

::You aren't like me. You are...an Instructor.:: The word came suddenly, and I rolled it around in my mind. What did it mean?

I found the barriers between me and my memories deep in my mind. I shattered them with a flick of my fingernail. I gasped as everything came flooding back. I recognized the people around me, and I knew where I was. Everything came back but the fear.

::I am a genetic anomaly,:: the thing countered, but its mind was full of lies. I could see the truth buried in its head. There were more Instructors. There were dozens of brothers and sisters, all bred from the same eggs.

It lunged for me, but I wasn't there. I'd moved before the thing could even finish planning its attack.

More memories came back to me—tools that helped me use my mind. Where were the blue lines that usually decorated my vision? I stepped out of the thing's way as it moved again, and it landed where I'd just been. I paid it no heed, too busy exploring myself to do more than notice it.

The blue lines hadn't gone anywhere. I pulled the visual representation of my mind up onto my field of vision and then banished it again. I didn't need those lines anymore. My mind did everything those lines used to do, only it was automatic. I was so much faster than I used to be.

I moved again as the thing thought of attacking. It howled in frustration. "Stand and fight, girl!"

I looked back at it, freezing its motion with a thought. "Is that what I am? Certainly, my biological chemistry resembles that of humankind, but do I act human?" I let down my shields and pulled her mind inside my own. ::Do I think like a human?:: I snapped my shields back up, expelling the other as something inside its mind broke and immobilizing terror flooded through its veins.

"You are human. You are *neurodivergent*. You have evolved past the idiot masses to see the world in a different light. Your mind is more powerful than any Turnip's weapon of war. You have the power we wish to give the Alpha-Superiors. You didn't think the Zetas were the end product, did you? It's this magical evolution. Do you really think my overlords would concern themselves with people as weak and stupid as you for any other reason?"

I felt the stench of fear wafting from the Instructor as it stood there, frozen.

Interesting. This thing that had once commanded fear was now afraid. Somehow, that was fitting.

I looked at the people scattered around. Most were still alive. The two telekinetics were sprawled on the floor, the box smashed into pieces and scattered around them. The telepath wasn't much farther. His mind was beginning to fail him. He hadn't been strong enough to tell the telekinetics that the thing had intended to hurt them. I reached out and grafted some of my gift into his mind so he could live. After all, that was what I was doing here, no? Protecting the lives of humans from those who wished them harm?

I pulled the other minds from their stupor and they began to awaken little by little.

::When you are gone, who will carry on your mission?:: I asked, and it halted its futile struggle against my grasp. I would release it when I wished, and not a second before.

::The traitor Defective will be brought before her siblings, and then we will continue the Harvest. Death will be gone as all are reborn as the Superior race. There are more like me, and they are coming. You won't survive this, girl.:: It hissed, but I wasn't interested in its words. I grasped the map of their bases and plucked it from her mind to examine it for myself. The thing was correct. There were sixteen more Instructors, each in its own position around the globe. I stored the map in my memory. It would be needed later.

"32, watch out!" Black shouted from behind me, where he was only now gaining consciousness.

::Do not be alarmed. It isn't a threat anymore—not now, anyway.:: But the warning brought the Instructor back to the forefront of my mind. Memories filtered through the cracks, reminding me of why I was here. Before Ms. King's tampering had fixed my mind, I had come to subdue her. Before, I had been fueled by feelings of betrayal, tempered by revenge. This thing had manipulated Houston into killing Mr. West, and had fed Briggs to the Institute to be changed. What would I do with it? I didn't want to kill it—I'd managed to get this far without any deaths on my conscience. But it couldn't be controlled by anyone else while it retained that much mental power. I closed my eyes and sent my mind careening inside the twisted pathways of Instructor neurology. It was structured much like the human mind, but there were portions that were designed to facilitate faster and heavier loads of processing. I pushed through the shields that encompassed it, trailing shards of shattered walls behind me as I explored.

There. I dug my mental fingers into the cluster and ripped it out. Ms. King didn't deserve that power. She couldn't control it all, anyway. If it wasn't useful, what was the point?

Pain flushed through the Instructor's body as it suddenly became mindblind. ::You will never hurt anyone again.:: I said coldly into its mind. It shuddered away with a whimper.

Just then, I heard a door open. Guns cocked around me. I bared my teeth in a cold smile as I reached out to their minds and froze them as well. If Ms. Green wished to speak with me, then she could do so without the threat of force.

::You are the one who has allowed the Institute to blind the Agency,:: I said as I sifted through her thoughts. I felt her intention and almost laughed. ::You want to kill me.:: Blinding fear and anger slashed though Ms. Green's consciousness. I dulled its bite as I sent feelers to assure myself that this woman was indeed human though and through.

That resolved, I allowed myself a cold laugh inside her mind. ::You are terrified of the power I hold. You believe my existence threatens the human race, and so you wish to destroy me. I suggest you rethink your options.::

Her thought frequencies shifted to show concern for the thing I held motionless with my thoughts. She catalogued the burns and slashes with ever mounting worry.

::Do not be concerned,:: I projected as her fear reached its peak in spite of my soothing. ::I have not killed it. It is simply unable to control itself in the same way your agents are incapable of firing their weapons.::

I finally opened my eyes and turned to face the Director of the Agency.

Ms. Green stood there, shock palpable on her face. "H-how can you—? You are rated PS7. No one has ever gotten through my shields."

::I suspect my rating no longer bears any relation to reality.:: I let the icy humor leak through into the projection.

Ms. Green's curiosity began to tint her fear.

::This thing is an Instructor created by the Institute. It is not a 'she', nor is it human—despite its looks. It is a human shell with everything that made it human scraped out and replaced with a monster.::

Ms. Green took a shaky step forward. "Is she dead?"

I chuckled. "What made it so powerful is now gone. It is just another Superior. Do with it what you will." The sound of my voice slid around my ears like an unanswerable question. Whatever had happened during that desperate fight for my mind had left my voice untouched. Strange.

I turned away to crouch over Tolden. Blood pounded through his veins with every beat of his heart as he struggled to piece his thoughts back together. *An angel,* his thoughts sighed as he peeled his eyes open. *Have you come to take me away?* I smiled and removed the wall I'd erected between myself and my emotions. As the pains from my injuries flooded through, so did my kindness.

::I am no angel, Carter Tolden.:: I projected it softly so it wouldn't scatter the drifting pieces of his mind. Then I reached out and guided his mind back to where it belonged. I felt his recognition as I stood back up.

"I have done what little I can for all of them," I said. I turned back to Ms. Green and spread my arms, palms out. Then slowly, I released the other agents. "Your medical facilities will have to offer them what I cannot."

Ms. Green nodded. "O-of course." Her mind was still not finished processing the scene in front of her, so I waited. Then her thoughts shifted as her eyes took time to consider the mix of agents on the floor. "I see your teammates." Ms. Green motioned to the rest of my team and then Ms. Graff. When her hand shifted to Smith, I recoiled. The memory of how Ms. King had ripped out her throat played behind my eyes. I hadn't felt a thing when she died. I hadn't even *recognized* her, and now she was dead. Now the Institute had taken two of my friends, and I hadn't been able to save either. Grief flooded in, hot and thick—combining with belated adrenaline to try and drown me. I held it at bay as best I could, but I couldn't stop the tears in my eyes.

"And you've thrown in with the Company." Ms. Green gestured to Hunt and Ms. Graff, who were beginning to stir. Ms. Green's thoughts hardened, but I smoothed away the sharp edges.

::The Company is here with me because the Institute is their enemy, too. They've extended their hand as allies. Please don't break what fragile peace we've created. You won't get another chance, and war between the Agency and Company is exactly what the Institute wants.::

I turned my thoughts to my shoulder as it sent another wave of agony through my mind. It wasn't life threatening unless it got infected—and the same was true of my broken nose and the slash across my abdomen I'd gotten from the thing's claws while I was battling in its mind.

Ms. Green nodded. The shock still wasn't gone from her system, but she'd managed to process the more important pieces of information.

One of the agents in tactical black leveled his gun at me.

I prepared to pull up the wall against my pain. If Ms. Green decided that she wanted a fight, then her agents wouldn't be able to even scratch me—but I didn't want it to come to blows again. I'd already lost too much today without hurting my fellow agents. Ms. Green was still in a stupor, and I could feel the incipient confusion rising in the agents with guns. They'd just heard her call me a traitor. Trigger fingers were getting itchy.

Rather than wait for it to boil over, I reached out and wiped the shock from Ms. Green's mind. Then I dumped everything I knew about the Superiors into her mind and withdrew.

The Director shook her head and looked up abruptly. "Agent 75, get these people to medical. Agent 2-83, lower your weapon." She looked me in the eye. "I don't know what you've done here, but don't think you're going to get away with it, *Agent*. I'm instructing you to surrender yourself for disciplinary action."

Agents rushed past me to help Hunt, Tolden and the others. They pulled those who couldn't walk from the floor and carried them back through the door. When all the injured agents were gone, I looked at the thing I held captive with my mind.

Ms. Green had asked me to surrender because she knew there was no way for her to actually take me down by force. Whatever had happened to my mind while I was fighting the Instructor had healed it. I no longer had to wait for my blue lines to process my surroundings, then react to the messages they sent me. If I wanted to, I could hold the whole room captive and walk away. Still, there was something Ms. Green didn't know. I didn't want to hurt anyone, and I never had. If I didn't surrender, then I would have to hurt more agents when they were inevitably sent to subdue me. At the end of the day, I'd known this was coming.

I had nothing against turning myself in. They'd trained me, and given me a home. The problem came with the Instructor that I still held in my grasp. I couldn't just release it. Nothing the Agency had could subdue it. Even with its gift neutralized, it was three times as powerful as the Superior we'd fought before. It would happily kill everyone in this room just to get to the Superior Medina held. I couldn't surrender and control the beast at the same time.

I closed my eyes against the throbbing pain in my muscles. "When I release this thing, it will attack—and no amount of physical pain or restraints will stop it. You thought bringing down D was difficult, but this one is different. It will not fall to the same mental attacks."

Ms. Green nodded. "Let it do its worse. My agents can handle it."

I frowned to myself, but released control of the Instructor and moved out of its reach. It turned immediately to lunge at the nearest tactical agent. It raked its claws up his back as it absorbed shot after shot from the others' handguns. His screams echoed like death in my ears. The agony in his cry aside, his injuries weren't life threatening—merely debilitating.

"That's enough." I dove back into its mind to stop it mere inches from the next agent's throat. "I told you that no amount of physical damage will stop it. This thing was created to destroy neurodivergents." I put it to sleep with a thought and watched as it crumpled to the ground. Then I put my hands behind my head. I'd done what I could. I didn't want to hurt these people. Now it was time to take my medicine.

I replaced the wall between me and my pain as I sank to my knees. Now was not the time to let emotions rule my mind. I'd done what I could to help them, but I had no illusions about the consequences. Black had spelled them out all too clearly at the overflow facility in D.C.. By taking control of the Instructor and the other agents, I had forfeited my place in the Agency. Now it was up to them.

EPILOGUE

I sat on the park bench admiring the trees as they swayed in the evening breeze. I couldn't feel their simple minds anymore—they were just out of reach. The transformation that had happened during my fight with Ms. King had been almost completely undone when they removed my biocard. My mind still moved faster—but the overwhelming mental power that had terrified both Ms. King and the Instructor was now gone. My abilities were shattered. My mental defenses were destroyed. I was everything but mindblind.

"I thought I would find you here."

It was Director Medina's voice. I could recognize it now. Sounds weren't as clear for me as they had been for Tabitha, but they were present. I felt a slash of pain as I thought about her. She was dead because of me.

"Yes. I do come here often. There isn't much else to do. School's out, and I've been fired from my job." I didn't even try to cover the ice in my voice. Part of me wanted to go home to Mom, but I knew deep down that I couldn't. The more exposure she had to the neurodivergent world, the faster her mind would burn. Dad had known that—I was sure that was part of the reason he'd left. Maybe he thought that, if he wasn't around, I wouldn't learn to use my psionic abilities and Mom would be safer for longer. Regardless, I couldn't be around Mom without hurting her, and I couldn't ask any of the neurodivergents I knew for help. My only chance of helping Mom was to find my father and demand answers. If he already knew about Mom's Instance, maybe he could help fix her.

Still, he could be anywhere, and I had no idea where to start looking. Going off half-cocked while the Agency was still in turmoil was a good way to get locked up, so I'd used the knowledge I'd gained from Ms. King's classes to steal another identity and holed up in a hotel room for the time being. I had enough money saved from my time at the Agency to stay there for a few months, if needed.

Medina chuckled as the sound of his footsteps in the grass grew closer. "Yes, I suppose we did fire you, didn't we?"

I slid over on the bench to allow him to sit. I ignored the Tactical agents I could hear behind the trees and see in the reflection of the cameras they'd installed to watch me. "If you have something to say, then say it."

Medina pulled a card out of his pocket. "I came to give you a warning—and an update on your team's condition."

I looked at him. "I'm listening."

"This is a card with two million dollars on it. You would be wise to take the money and disappear." I took the card, and Medina pressed a second package into my hand. "The Company and the Agency have convened talks to decide how to deal with the Institute—that much is public knowledge. What they aren't saying is that the Agency has discovered major Institute tampering inside the upper echelons. If the corruption runs too deep, we won't be able to salvage the Agency. Ms. Green is in favor of merging the Agency with the Company to create one Organization, and I have a feeling that you aren't far away from being on one of the kill-lists once the Company's Director takes the reins. You'll need these."

"What?" I slammed the gate down on my emotions, and my senses sharpened as I started to calculate the possibilities.

Medina's lips thinned. "The Agency has been infiltrated once. What's to keep it from happening again? A detailed audit has revealed that the Institute has been covertly bankrolling over half our operations. When you attacked Ms. King, you cost a lot of people money and effectively destroyed the

Agency as you knew it. We can't just dissolve. That would let too many neurodivergents loose into society—which would do more harm than good unless we can screen every single person for Institute tampering. Beside that, we've promised stable employment to half a million people."

"So you're creating a fresh Organization designed to combat the Institute. I understand that much. But why are you coming after me?" I hated that plaintive note in my voice— but hadn't I given these people enough already without letting them hunt me down like an animal?

"Well, to be honest, there are a lot of people in the Company who think you're more dangerous than the Institute. Your display of power back there didn't go unnoticed. Also, in the four months you were with the Agency, you jumped our research and development programs ahead by three years. They don't want you selling to the highest bidder—not even in purely Turnip settings."

I grit my teeth. "What about my mom? Does she need to disappear too?" If they went after her when I left to find my dad, I would never forgive myself.

Medina's eyes softened. "Adalind Farina should be safe enough. We will watch her, but that's more to protect her from the Institute, than the Organization."

I breathed a sigh of relief, and returned my attention to the card in my hand. "I'm not stupid. The card will be traced, and I will be found the moment I use the money."

"Yes, if you use that card. The money is transferable to any account you want. I'm sure Ms. King has given you a comprehensive tutorial on how to make money like that disappear."

I frowned. "You really want me out of your city, don't you?"

He smiled bitterly. "No, but there are others who do. Your friends are recovering, and they will be allowed the choice of whether or not to continue their work with the Organization.

The Company agents are up and about, and Tabitha Smith's funeral will be tomorrow. Agent Hunt asked me to extend an invitation to you. She said you were the only one conscious when Agent Smith died."

I winced as he said Tabitha's name. The memory of my confusion as Ms. King tore out her throat was all too fresh in my mind. I hadn't felt anything at the time—hadn't even recognized her.

"It wasn't your fault," he said softly. "You're the only reason we're all alive."

My head snapped around. "Then why did you take my bio-card?" All the anger and frustration came out, and more than one plasma weapon cycled to readiness behind the trees.

Medina's expression drew cold. "You gave classified information to enemy agents, you attacked a teacher, and you aided in the escape of a prisoner. You're lucky we didn't take you to a back alleyway somewhere and shoot you. But here you are, still alive. I was kind."

"No." Something in his sentence was very wrong. I retraced his words in my mind.

Medina cocked his head. "No?"

"No," I repeated. "What prisoner?"

Medina didn't bother to hide his confusion. "The Superior we captured—D—is gone. I assumed you had merely neglected to tell me about that portion of your plan."

It took a moment to click, but I allowed myself a smile when it did. "She's out there somewhere now, huh?" With the Instructor gone, she was free to continue sabotaging the Institute.

"We've ordered an Agency wide search, but—"

"—No. Let her go. She's where she can do the most good." I slipped my rings back onto my fingers. "It's your choice, really, but she seems better suited to independent operations, and we need all the help we can get." Then I stood and pulled my newest creation off my belt. "Thanks for the update—and the warning. You might as well take the camera down, I'm not coming back anytime soon."

I fired the device and held tight as I flew through the air to land soundly on top of a nearby tree. I fired it a second time and made the top of the next building. I tucked the card into my pocket and turned the second package over to read the back.

"I'm listening -Carter Tolden," was all it said. I placed the card into my pants pocket and ripped open the package. It was a semiautomatic—the same one he'd had Black give me after we'd brought Houston in.

A smile caressed my face as I closed my eyes to focus what was left of my tattered gift. There, in the distance, I could feel him standing and thinking my name as loud as he could. I pushed the gun into the holster I still wore strapped to my thigh.

::Thank…you.::

THANK YOU

Dear Reader,

Thank you for taking the time to read Crystal Choice. I hope you enjoyed Crystal's journey.

Before you go, please take a moment to leave a review of my book. Tell me what you liked, what you loved, and even what you hated—I just want to hear what you think. Reviews aren't easy to come by, which means that you—the reader—have the power to help Crystal's story reach the people who most need to hear it. Here's a link to my author page, which includes all my books on Amazon:

amazon.com/author/kaexcell

Thank you again for spending time with Crystal. I hope to meet you again between the pages of another book!

Sincerely,

K. A. Excell

LOOKING FOR MORE?

Join the mailing list at KAExcell.com to learn more about new releases.

COMING SOON: CRYSTAL TRUTH

ABOUT THE AUTHOR

K. A. Excell uses her experiences gained from growing up in an autism-rich household to create a world where Neurodivergence really is a superpower. She blends her years of martial arts study with the complexities of Autism Spectrum Disorder to create a world with realistic characters and challenges. She lives in Utah.